PRAISE FOR THE WRITING OF TROY BLACKLAWS

Karoo Boy

"*Karoo Boy* is told in the voice of a spectacularly original young male protagonist who in his own way is as captivating and memorable as Holden Caulfield."
  —John Berendt, author of *Midnight in the Garden of Good and Evil*

"A beautifully evocative coming-of-age story."
  —Bryce Courtenay, author of *The Power of One*

"The most colorful book I have ever read."
  —Chris Martin, lead singer of Coldplay

Blood Orange

"*Blood Orange* is an important, vital voice to add to the tapestry of literature coming out of Southern Africa. Such vibrancy is rare in any literature. Coming out of such a legacy of violence and pain, it is nothing less than a miracle."
  —Alexandra Fuller, author of *Don't Let's Go to the Dogs Tonight*

"Troy Blacklaws beautifully lays bare how it took raw guts for a young white boy to resist apartheid."
  —Antjie Krog, author of *Country of My Skull*

"Tantalizingly beautiful."   —Desmond Tutu

Cruel Crazy Beautiful World

"The words immediately took me into the world of the novel and made me look in a fresh way into the room behind the eyes."
—Witi Ihimaera, author of *The Whale Rider*

"*Cruel Crazy Beautiful World* beautifully chronicles the hazardous fates of the scatterlings that immense historical waves leave on the beach."
—Phillip Noyce, director of *Rabbit-Proof Fence* and *The Quiet American*

"Bold, poetic, terrifying."
—Terry Westby-Nunn, author of *The Sea of Wise Insects*

"Mesmerizing and evocative. I am in awe."
—Deon Meyer, author of *Blood Safari* and *Trackers*

Cruel Crazy
Beautiful
World

Cruel Crazy Beautiful World

A Novel

TROY BLACKLAWS

OPEN ROAD
INTEGRATED MEDIA
NEW YORK

Cover design by Barbara Brown

ISBN 978-1-4804-1781-6

This edition published in 2013 by Open Road Integrated Media
345 Hudson Street
New York, NY 10014
www.openroadmedia.com

for Daniela

Bows

Johnny Clegg for letting me snatch words from his song. Peter Godwin for casting an eye over Zimbabwe storyline. Isobel Dixon, Scott Eddington, Jason Hinojosa, Andrew MacDonald and James Scorer for reading pencil-in-hand. Lisa C. for her deft editing and Megan Southey at Jacana for proofreading. Nigel Gwynne-Evans for being my sherpa on Table Mountain. Anderson Tepper, Chris Crutcher, Cindy Hood, John Johnson, Juliet, Leon Kandelaars, Zakes Mda, Micha, Geoff Roberts, Helena Spring, Joshua Sternlicht, Tim Volem for their faith in my storytelling. Craig Morris and Greig Coetzee for lending my words wings. Hugh Masekela, and Bafo Bafo for magic tunes.

Cruel Crazy
Beautiful
World

It's a cruel crazy beautiful world . . .

— JOHNNY CLEGG & SAVUKA

1

Cape Town. December 2004.

A boy tracks a skinny dun cow along a caged footbridge over the N2 highway out of town. The bridge is wired in to keep crazy cows from jumping and bitter boys from dropping bricks onto motorcars that shark along the tarmac below. For such boys Mandela's longed-for freedom is a joke.

A haze of smoke and summer dust hangs low over Crossroads shantytown.

Behind us the sun hovers over Table Mountain.

On the roadside a tow truck, like a morbid mantis, dreams up its next victim.

And on the radio Miles Davis blows high, cicada notes.

See my old man with a lazy palm on the wheel of his mystic-green '74 Benz and his other hand combing his ducktail. Zero Cupido: in his faring Hawaiian shirt and snakeskin boots, he looks the part of a dodgy Cuban dealer in an American film. In fact he's half Cape Malay, half Cuban. With just a jot of Hottentot blood. In theory he's Muslim. In reality he loves his whisky and pig and hasn't gone to mosque for a long time. He has no intent to go on *Hajj*, yet he enjoys orientating his life to Mecca. He draws an arrow in the sand with his foot whenever he's on a beach. He has pencilled an arrow under the roof of the veranda. Ghosting through Cape Town, he'll cast his eyes starwards to find south and then figure out the angle to Mecca. That imaginary notch in his mind *keeps the world from spinning too randomly*, he tells me.

Now, out of the blue, Zero's put his snakeskinned foot down. *Jero, the freeloading's over*, he said to me. He'll no longer fork out *good money* (?!) on a son who is *a drifter and a dreamer: forever lolling on the harbour wall, forever sipping cocktails with flaky gay artists, forever writing sappy po-ems.* He spat out the word *poems* as he might a litchi stone. He has no time for *fucking daffodils dancing in the breeze.* It's unclear whether he is recycling the one line of poetry he recalls from his school days, or is calling all poets and other artists *daffodils.*

My old man sees himself as a realist. He endlessly waxes his Benz, fills his hands with a whore's tits, slices kudu *biltong* against his thumb, douses his fish and chips in vinegar, turns sizzling chops with his bare fingers and licks them off. He has zero finesse at the bone. His idea of fine-tuning is running a kind of spit cloth through the barrel of his Colt 45, or measuring and adjusting the gap in his spark plug. He wants the spark to jump far . . . so it *burns clean.*

I silently scorn his world of dabbling and dealing, of whistling at schoolgirls in skimpy skirts and shooting pool in murky bars, of totting up takings on a Lion matchbox and smoking fat Havana cigars.

It's a mystery to Zero how I'm so tuned into the ephemeral, into things neither here nor there. I'm fazed by the sound of old men sucking air through gaps in their teeth. I sniff the wispy smoke from under a just-unlidded beer bottle as if it is perfume. I love Parma ham shaved in opaque slivers. I linger in a cinema long after a film ends to ride out the vibe as long as I can. I enjoy arthouse films with their *zen* endings that hang in midair. I gaze into a lava lamp until I see flamingos and phantoms. I listen to indie folk and whimsical garage instead of hard rock. All this renders me a *moffie* in his eyes. A free-verse fairy with a footloose soul.

He has a point. I still have zip on paper after two years of reading for my thesis on García Márquez at the University of Cape Town. I got lost in the dusty labyrinth of his Latin American mind. All the thoughts I placed on paper somehow became poems . . . and a play. *Lost?* This is beyond imagining for Zero. He never goes beyond the Cape Flats without a map in hand. He loves to unfold a road map and follow the N2 all the way to Durban with a finger. Then to laugh at my fumbling bid to origami the map along the original folds again. Ironic, for a man of such hazy ethics to be so focused on compass points in a land where booming shantytowns render maps old overnight.

I curse him for exiling me to survive all alone out in Hermanus: boondock harbour town south-east of Cape Town. *Hermaanus*. I hope you've never heard of it.

We go by a fire raging on a highway island. A wizardy old man shakes a fly whisk at the flames.

My amigos pity me. At dusk today they'll all head down to the Cape Town harbour for sundowners. They'll jabber their dreams of recording music and put forward their beer-foam theories on why Mandela's rainbow dream fell out of focus in this land of antithesis. And where will I be? In Hermanus, other side of Hangklip, far from the jazzy verve of Cape Town.

7

– My father and my father's father were fishermen in Kalk Bay, Zero intones. Jero, my boy, you come from a long line of fishermen.

He swivels his focus away from the Benz icon to glare unblinking eyes at me, to spook me out.

This is, I think, his bid to prove the futility and absurdity of my reading García Márquez.

– But Dad, this sea's been fished dry and the fishermen are dying out. Besides, my other grandfather taught philosophy.

He taught in Vienna until 1937. Then he sailed for Cape Town. He was one of the few lucky Jews. Lucky to have eluded the Nazis then. Lucky too to have keeled over before his daughter fell for a Muslim.

Zero flicks my words out the wound-down window with his ducktailing hand.

– And he had to sell newspapers to put a roof over his head when he came out to Cape Town. Philosophy won't put fish and a beer in your hands. I tell you flat, my boy, if you want to survive . . . you have to have something to trade.

That's Zero's Survival Tip #1.

He'll hand you his hard-earned wisdom free of charge. One hand palm up (as if balancing the circle of the wheel) and the other with fingers down (tapping on his drum-taut gut), he may just remind you of Buddha calling on the earth to witness his moment of illumination.

I look away out my window and see four nude youths on the rim of the road: painted from head to foot in white clay, they perch on the roof of a gutted motorcar. I catch the thudding of a boom-box bass and see their eyes pan after us.

They linger in my mind long after they fade in the rearview. The white clay renders them invisible to the spirits who want to waylay them during this hazardous limbo time when they're no longer cowherding, lizard-catching boys and not yet men.

In the past, when they verged on manhood, Xhosa boys would be sent out of their mother's hut far into the untamed *bundu* to learn to survive by hunting and foraging. You'd never see them during the in-between time. Now there's hardly any *bundu* left and the only wild animals are tourist-hustling baboons, feral dogs and cocky rats. Each day another row of shanty huts is conjured out of the dust of dying, dwindling *bundu*. And each day folk stray further and further out to seek firewood.

Zero takes the exit for the Strand. Bullet holes scar the sign. This is a surreal Nevada rather than the Nirvana foretold.

Apartheid depended on static, unequivocal signposts. Nowadays signs shift all the time. Words on them fade, or hang skew after kamikaze taxivans wipe out a post. They become shanty roofs or, flipped, advertise a barbershop or a shebeen or second-hand coffins. Even roadside milestones get pinched to hold down canvas tents in the southeaster banshee-wind. Names of the dead vanish from graveyards, the brass letters traded for drug money. The time when words stood still on poles is long gone. Words just won't stay put.

– But *you* don't catch fish, Dad, I dare shoot back at Zero after the long lull.

This too is scripted. I find holes in his logic and he just shifts the focus.

– I trade in other things.

– And one day they'll put you in jail.

Zero laughs. He levels his eyes at me again and taps his forehead.

– I'm too savvy for them, my boy.

Then he winks slyly.

– I leave no spoor. No proof.

He blows air through fluttering lips. His shot at drama falls flat. You'd think he'd ditch the theatrics with me. I'm not duped by his act. His mates, on the other hand, hang on his quips and tips as if he's a god.

His mates being his sidekicks: Canada Dry and Dove Bait. Men who'd die for him, he loves to tell me. There's always a sulky hint that I would not.

He'd found a job in the dry docks for Canada Dry, that jackass of a dope-dealer, when he came out of jail.

For Dove Bait, cocky Casanova of the Cape Flats, he'd found a doctor to hook out a girlfriend's unloved foetus with a bent bicycle spoke.

And then there's another mate of his he'd hid in our attic for two years after he ran his foe Black Mamba down dead in the taxi wars. In his case it's harder to tell how he reads Zero. He's flinty and taciturn. He survived in the attic on tinned sardines and books I took out of the university library for him. He got hooked on Freud. When he ventured out again, he shaved his head bald to elude Black Mamba's boys, had *Phoenix* tattooed on his forehead and juggled *tingalinging* Chinese Baoding balls in one palm. The old, upbeat taximan they called Bahaya was dead. Instead we had an iguana-eyed backyard guru in a faded pink Lacoste shirt who could dart a sparrow out of our lemon tree with his blowpipe.

Canada Dry, forever spaced out on grass, would jibe that the blowpipe was a *ganja* bong from the Congo and that it was as long as Dove Bait's dong. Phoenix alone never cracks jokes, is never bawdy. He hears all their tall macho tales with a wry smile in a corner of his lips. Sometimes he gives me a conniving wink. He's even-keeled and *zen* as a spirit level. And yet I imagine he too would die for Zero.

– No proof, echoes Zero.

– So you'd rather I become a crook than a poet?

– You piss on the hand that feeds you, Jerusalem.

Zero spits gob at the wind. His calling me by my full name is a sign he's riled.

– Besides, in other countries you can freely trade the things I sell. The law's fickle. Yesterday's jailbirds are today's heroes in this crazy land. What's black market now you'll find in the 7-Eleven tomorrow.

He puts his foot on the gas to go past a smoking, tilting taxivan. A *Zola Budd*. As we go by we hear the squawk of chickens in a cage on the taxi roof.

Zero wags his trigger finger at me.

– Just remember this. This *crook* money put you through university. And you still beg for pocket money whenever you go out.

I just keep my eyes on the road ahead.

At the Strand a black dog lopes along the sand. A longboarder rides the foam.

I remember Miriam, my mother, scolding my father for going too far out to sea with me. He'd bait and cajole till the sand fell away and I doggy-paddled. He thought I was scared of the deep. I never told him I was scared of sharks, for he would have called me a *moffie*. My mother was not as far gone then. She'd stay huddled in the Benz and doodle on the margins of the newspaper till they became a mosaic of mermaids and turtles and nude girls. Or she'd sit on a sarong on the sand and peel a mandarin and flip the peels into my father's snakeskin boots.

She still taught girls how to paint on silk, then. And she still coloured her lips.

– One day I'll find a way of surviving by the pen.

– Survive, hey? By writing *po-ems*? Tell me then, what does a *po-em* fetch in the market?

This from the man who once told me magical stories out of his head. How did he end up so money-minded and arid?

A Chevy Silverado pickup rides hard on our tail.

– How much will folk fork out for a fresh metaphor, hey? And will you mark down one that's fingered? Or does it flower, like an opal or a pussy, if you handle it?

Just so, my old man, unwittingly, uses poetry to put down poetry.

The Silverado flashes his headlights at us to shift left so he can zoom by.

Zero, glancing in the rearview, stays in his groove.

The Silverado hoots.

Zero flicks him a finger. No Silverado cowboy is going to hustle him off the road.

The Silverado hoots again.

Zero just laughs.

Opals. Another sideline of his. Along with uncut diamonds.

As for the other thing, an image of my sallow mother floats into my mind. Zero never goes out with her. There was a time when he had had to hide his white-skinned girl behind a veil. And the taboo had spiced their romance. She'd wear a slit-eyed burka to the beach and a Malay head cloth to the drive-in. The law forbade them to marry, so they went to Amsterdam. After Mandela came out of jail, they came home to Cape Town with my sister and me as mementos of their exile. And in Mandela's rainbow land they no longer had to dodge and dive . . . but by then their love had run dry. And folk no longer saw flicks at the drive-in.

While Zero cruises all over the Cape, my mother haunts the front yard, mumbling to her gnomes arcane words I am hard put to decipher. If she's not communing with her gnomes she's drifting in a dream.

Just ahead of us a surfboard flies off the roof rack of a jeep. It flick-flacks on the tarmac.

Zero swings hard to dodge it.

2

Limpopo river.

Just as a rogue surfboard scratches paint off a Silverado far to the south, Jabulani Freedom Moyo surfaces from the muddy Limpopo that runs from Botswana to Mozambique and forms the border between Zimbabwe and South Africa.

As he runs along a bald footway under a power line, he reflects on how he became a fugitive.

Not that long ago he was still an English teacher at a high school in Bulawayo, in the Ndebele southlands. In the afternoons he coached cross-country, javelin, long jump and football. Though he cursed all the marking of papers, he loved the upbeat dialogue with his students.

One day, over tea in the staffroom, he'd remarked to his colleagues that Mugabe looked like a joker in his vivid, Java-print shirts

– West African style. They had laughed. They felt no love for that Shona man who had commandeered their country. But one rat had felt it his duty to report him to the headmaster.

The headmaster (a Shona posted to Bulawayo by Mugabe) had made Jabulani stand up in front of all the schoolchildren in the school hall when he read out the crime (mocking Mugabe) and the verdict from Harare: Mister Moyo was fired. The headmaster had reminded his school that Mugabe was taught by Jesuits and had studied overseas and was therefore no joker. He'd said Mister Moyo was lucky not to be jailed.

Students and teachers had dared to hiss at the injustice of a teacher being shot down over a jibe. It was not as if Mister Moyo had tossed darts at the image of Mugabe, or had not stood still as Mugabe went by in his Benz convoy. If schoolboys in Bulawayo had learnt one thing, it's this: in Zimbabwe the law is just a *panga* blade to cut down Mugabe's foes.

The irony is that Mugabe had once been Jabulani's hero in the *chimurenga*, the long fight for freedom. Jabulani had spent his boyhood bowing to the White Man in Rhodesia. He was halfway through high school when Mugabe had outfooted that old white Smith. Rhodesia was now Zimbabwe and Salisbury now Harare. And it was in this free Zimbabwe that Jabulani Freedom Moyo had become a human being who held his head up high.

But then the rumours had begun to bleed out. Of killings in the Ndebele south. Of corpses dumped down an old mineshaft. Of the raping of girls. Of white farmers run off farms that Mugabe then doled out to his mates. Of starving, uprooted farmhands camping in roadside gullies. And, in the end, the *jambanja*, the chaos of being tossed out, went beyond the farms and you saw the fugitives on the pavements in town holding quavering chickens and skinny goats and peanuts in Castrol cans.

Teachers had looked up from their newspaper or coffee when Jabulani had gone into the staffroom to empty his pigeonhole. Someone (the rat?) had posted a dry, flat frog in it. Teachers had defied the scowls of the Shona headmaster and stood and tapped their teaspoons against their teacups in a staccato tattoo of camaraderie. For Jabulani they risked their feet being beaten and their heads being *submarined* by a gang of Mugabe's goons.

A student of his had come to his classroom to tell him that he'd learnt a myriad things in his class and that he now wanted to become a writer. He'd learnt how to tune in to the music of words. The boy had hidden his tears behind a hand and Jabulani had hugged him and put a Hemingway in his other hand. A book about a jinxed old fisherman was a curious gift to a boy who might never see the sea.

As Jabulani put his books and pens into a cardboard box, he had thought Zimbabwe's hard-earned freedom was just like that giant marlin the old man took so long to reel in. And now it was being ravaged by sharks. But in this case the fisherman did not fend off the sharks that zeroed in on his catch. He too was hacking the fish down to its bare bones. That was what was so warped.

On the way out of school the headmaster had waylaid him and rifled through the box in Jabulani's hands to see for himself whether Jabulani was not perhaps pinching a hole-punch or an Oxford dictionary. If Jabulani ran his country's ruler down there was no telling how low he would go, was the headmaster's parting shot.

Jabulani had taught at the school for fourteen years.

From then on he was a marked man and no school would hire him.

Hearing his old Datsun blow up one night, he'd run out into the strung-up corpse of the family's cat.

They had painted VIVA MUGABE on the walls in cat blood.

Then he'd landed a job in a bicycle shop called Cheap John's

Cycle Repair. But they had burnt it down and Cheap John had blamed Jabulani for his misfortune. In a town where a synagogue had burnt out less than a year before, the police hardly noted the end of a bicycle shop. That was in June.

And for half a year now there'd been no meat to go with the half loaf of bread he'd stood in line for each afternoon. For half a year they had survived off the pittance his wife, Thokozile, earned as a nurse. For half a year his son and daughter had stared at him, wondering when he'd pull a rabbit out of the hat to recall the magic of the past.

Back then he'd come home high on football fever and down a beer on the front step while the cat licked his salty shins. He'd clap his hands as his son Panganai played guitar or beatboxed and his daughter Tendai hula-hooped or cartwheeled. In his pockets he'd have a guitar pick for Panganai and a hairpin for Tendai. And, after another quart or two of beer, he'd flirt with Thokozile, flipping up her skirt to pinch her ass.

Then he'd lost his post and all the fat and fun of his world had been pared away.

– You have to run away from that *gandanga* Mugabe, that murderer, Thokozile had said while rats fidgeted in the roof overhead.

The rats had got out of hand since the cat died.

– He will hunt you, that fucking *gandanga*. And he will kill you. Just as he will kill anyone, Shona or not, who is his foe.

– How can I go?

– You have to, otherwise we hunger to the bone. Now, before Christmas, is a good time to go to South Africa. All tourists from overseas go to Cape Town for Christmas holidays and they have money in their pockets. You will find a job and send us money.

– Where will I stay?

– Other men find a way. You may be so lucky and find a job in a bar where they put a roof over your head.

Though she'd cajoled him in this way, she'd never blamed him for the way things had panned out. She'd never reminded him that a dumb, flippant joke of his had cursed them. Though he no longer flirted so cockily, she'd still lured him to her in the dark, telling him he'd always be her man. And after their loving he'd blow cool wind from his lips along the scalp-skin furrows between her cornrows.

And it was not just her. The holes in Panganai's Pumas told him he had to go. The faded, let-down hem of Tendai's school skirt told him he had to go. The empty breadbox told him he had to go. A stone through the kitchen window told him he had to go. The bark of stray dogs as he lay awake at night told him he had to go. Somehow he had to find a life for them beyond this rat-riddled madness of starving and scavenging, of fearing and flinching.

Yet he was dead scared of heading south.

He'd heard of the crocodiles and the undertow in the Limpopo.

He'd heard of border soldiers on the far bank of the Limpopo who'd shoot you and hide your corpse rather than deal with the paperwork to deport you.

He'd heard of the *gumagumas*: roving, raping swindlers who lurk in the *bundu* and hoodwink your money out of you.

He'd heard of vigilante South African farmers who ride pickups through the borderlands and shoot at stray Zimbabweans. The farmers blame them for the looting and random murders. In the old days the border had been guarded by drafted white-boy soldiers. Now there is no draft in South Africa and the borders are riddled with holes.

He's heard from the deported that in a border town called Musina a police captain has photos of dead refugees on file. This girl called Jendaya was raped and stabbed by the *gumagumas*. They found her with her panties on her head. This boy called Goodwill was robbed and stabbed by the *gumagumas*. In his pocket was a paper in the hand of his schoolteacher, pleading for pills to cure his mother of the blood in her spit.

He had no money for the *malaishas*, the human smugglers (half upfront, half on arrival). He had no friend in Cape Town to shack up with till he found his feet.

If he survived crocodiles and soldiers, *gumagumas* and vigilantes, and somehow got a ride to Cape Town, then he'd need to beg for asylum papers from Home Affairs. And until he had papers he'd have to dodge the Nigerians in this place and the Tanzanians in that place, the Gambians here and the Kenyans there. He'd have to skirt the townships where black South Africans blamed *dirty* Zimbabweans for pinching their jobs and their girls and for dabbling in witchcraft.

Yet he's lucky he's a man, for they may just give him asylum. They give no papers to boys and girls, so they have to survive in limbo. The boys camp under bridges, in roadside culverts and on outskirt dumps of junk and dirt. You see them (if you have eyes to look) in their ratty shorts and tacky flip-flops scavenging in bins, plucking at guitars conjured from paraffin tins, playing football with a dirty tennis ball, dodging motorcars to beg as the robots go from orange to red. Ether from a bottle of glue may send them on blurred, spinning trips. The girls you never see. They morph into maids, wives and whores. Never mermaids.

An aeroplane hums overhead. Jabulani detours from the path to shinny up an acacia tree.

His heart still beats hard long after the humming of the plane fades out.

Once dark falls he will head further south through this foreign veld pervaded by cackling calls, distant shots and jaggy-tooth things.

3

Hermanus. Midafternoon.

The town sulks under a smudged sky, caught between stoic mountains and a grey sea.

Zero spots a half-hidden white pickup up ahead and his foot rides light on the pedal.

– Pigs, Zero spits.

Zero has hated the police since they loaded up the alley-striped, jazz-pervaded world of his boyhood in District Six onto the flatbed of a truck and shifted his family to a matchbox house out on the windswept Cape Flats. He had seen his father go from finger-snapping, nipple-pinching, banjo-strumming charmer to a mumbling ghost within half a year of the bulldozers levelling the jumbled bars and haunts of a jaunty, jiving youth. His father died a muted, bitter death in a randomly wired-off zone out on the dusty Flats.

Me, I am free to come and go despite being half *coloured.* Yet I fear for this land where a blood-lusting *tsotsi* will stab an old man with a flick knife for the pittance in his pocket, where Mbeki (our tea-sipping chief) turns a blind eye to the *loco* antics of Mugabe just over the border, and where Zuma (Mbeki's second fiddle) is somehow above the law. There are murmurs in the papers of dodgy arms deals and pocketed money. Yet they can't catch Zuma out. He's as elusive as a chameleon that shuffles his camo colours at whim.

My old man, however, revels in this loophole-riddled time.

The Benz halts in front of the scuba-diving shop on the seafront road.

The sea scatters foam like white feathers of shot birds.

Along the rocks an old man furtively knifes mussels out of cracks.

A gummy-eyed old hobo herds his reeking, bagged world on a hospital gurney. The gurney's wheels squeal like cornered rats.

– You happen to have a fag? Or a bob or two? Either will do.

Zero fishes a packet of Camels out of the pocket of his half-mast Dockers. He finds a balled ten-rand note in his pocket. He fingers out two smokes.

The hobo tucks one behind his ear and puts the other between his cracked lips. He fattens out the note, holds it up to squint at the watermark like some wary dealer, then folds it and tucks it behind his hat band.

Zero rummages in the Benz's cubbyhole for an old Bic lighter and hands it to the hobo.

His fag catches fire, then fades to a glow.

– Ta for the fire.

Now the hobo studies the orange Bic lighter lying in his red-lined, dirt-rimed hand.

– It's yours, chirps Zero.

The hobo nods ta, and thumbs down the gas to sniff at it.

Zero fetches a can of oil out of the boot. Then he kills that ratty squealing of the gurney.

That's the thing with my old man. Just when you peg him as an asshole, he off-foots you.

Over the roof of the shop a great white shark gapes its jaw at a dummy in a wetsuit in a diving cage.

Half of Zero's left calf is gone from the time a shark took him while he was diving for crayfish. He had gone on diving for years after to prove to his mates that he was *no moffie.* Nowadays others dive for him . . . for the sacks of crayfish traded in alleyways behind pubs. Another of his sideline capers: purveyor of pirated shellfish.

We lug my guitar and a kit bag (full of bunged-in Levis and rugby jerseys) and banana boxes (full of studied novels with un- lined spines, curiously devoid of pencil marks and coffee stains) and Johnnie Walker boxes (full of Zero's *trading goods*) up a flight of whining steps.

On the landing, while I fiddle with the key, he randomly picks up a book from one of the boxes.

– How the hell can you read a book and not crack the spine? It's unnatural.

Again I find this ironic, coming from the man who leaves no spoor. I merely shrug as he flicks through the book.

In fact I never annotated my textbooks at university. I never inked my name on the flyleaf. I never took notes in lectures. I just tuned in and remembered. I have that kind of mind. I remember things.

– You think you're higher than your old man now you've read all your books, hey?

He drops the book.

– I tell you, life is too short for highfalutin books with long words.

The door swings open. Light filters through a salt-filmed window into the spartan flat. A smell of dust and flat beer and old record sleeves flows out.

A sagging bed stands on paint-flecked floorboards. A half-blind mirror hovers over a basin. A rickety bentwood chair lurks under a graffitied desk. A blade fan drops a dirty string. A bare bulb dotted with fly shit dangles at the end of a wire.

I flick the switch and the bulb flares, illuminating flecks of mosquito blood on the walls.

Zero tugs the string of the fan. The blades sigh into a blur.

Through the window I see the new harbour a mile away, across the bay.

On a random nail I hang a watercolour my mother once did of a seagull in Kalk Bay harbour. I found the painting folded up in a book long after she burnt the others. Long after she put a diamond ring and all her milky opals in a drawer for good.

Over time my mother traded the company of men for her front-yard gnomes. She loves her gnomes for wanting nothing from her other than the pigeon shit wiped off their glossy red hats. She loves their jolly mouths rimmed in snowy white for being forever amused by her mutterings. They never burp beer fumes at her. Nor do they leer at other women. *Mazel tov* is all they ever say. *Lucky star.* Yet the stars have not been kind to her. In their mouths *mazel tov* is just another way of saying *such is life*.

She can't bear the way Zero licks his fingers to turn the page when he reads the paper, nor his tacky spinal tattoo of a mango-titted virago, nor his habit of flicking fag stubs into her fuchsias, nor the way he foots her Bengal cat aside. While he's out cruising after dusk she dozes off in front of her murder mysteries with her cat in her lap, never seeing the killer caught. Or she studies the neat hole left in an avocado by the pip, until it begins to tint sepia. Then she spoons it into her mouth, happy that she no longer has to worry about him smearing her lipstick with whisky-fumed lips.

Phoenix has a theory that my mother's so hooked on murder mysteries because she gets to vicariously kill Zero over and over again. And that old Zero's in the dark about this.

Perhaps Zero and my mother are still tenuously twinned in this knack for never being caught red-handed.

All the years I studied at university neither my mother nor her opals were rubbed to draw their fire to the surface. She exudes so stoic and islanded an aura that I seldom hold her, the woman who bears the shimmering scars of my unfurling in her womb. The woman whose milk I sucked and who read *Alice in Wonderland* to me as she tucked me in at night.

I sigh at not having to witness my mother drift ever further into her wordless, wary, gnomic world. Or to catch her again in the dark on grass all blue with fallen jacaranda flowers, lying fat and naked and deathly white, as if raped by the moon.

Though Zero's a dog, I have to confess there's something of his eye for girls in me. My heart skips a beat when the southeaster flips up the skirt of a stockinged girl. I too have gawped at the copper hips and jiggling moons of the Loop Street go-go girls. And yet my old man's lip-licking at the sight of a scant skirt renders me somehow ashamed of being a man.

Am I a man, then? Is a man as scared of the random hop of frogs as I am? Does a man blow *kazoooing* bubbles through a straw in the lees of a mojito? Does a man cry freely during a film? Does a man just let his mother fade out? Does a man bow to his old man's plan for him instead of heading out into the world to seek his fortune?

I feel like a white-clay boy who has been exiled from his mother's hut to wander ghost-like through the *bundu* till I become a man. This time now, in this boondocks place, is my *bundu* time. It may not be hard-core *bundu*, I may not have to kill things or dig up roots, but it is nevertheless where I'll have to learn to survive alone. I'd rather just play my guitar and whimsically pen poems, maybe travel to see the world: Galway, Sienna, Malacca, Saigon, Mandalay. Yet I feel I have to undergo this exile if I am ever to free myself from my old man.

A hidden gecko chirps at this daunting thought.

Zero listlessly plucks a few strings of my guitar. You can hear that the feeling for it is still in his fingers though he hasn't played his guitar for years, ever since the thing that can never be undone happened.

I fling the window ajar. I look out over the sweep of Walker Bay. I smell a fusion of salt and rotting kelp and seagull guano. Feathery wave froth fuses with white sky.

The world lies under a skin of dust. Sounds warp as if played on a tape left too long in the sun. Wind gusts off the sea, chucking scraps of paper about.

I pick up a flyer advertising pizza.

Two gaunt black dogs hide from the wind in a capsized forty-gallon drum in a corner of the empty market square. They curl floppy pink lips to flash their canines at us.

Zero squints at a flapping map of the market layout to find his bearings.

The dogs eye us through lacklustre eyes.

There is the Burgundy restaurant on the west of the square. The Fisherman's Cottage pub is behind him, so my stall (he figures out) is to be just in front of this low white wall. Under this kaffir plum, right here.

He folds the map away and Zippos a Camel in the lee of his hand.

I look at the space that is to become my world. The measure of a jail cell. In the shade of this kaffir plum I am to sell bead animals made by wizard-fingered Zimbabweans in Cape Town while fellow refugees hold their place in the never-ending line for asylum papers.

– The bead animals will sell like hotcakes. The good beadwork is done by the Zimbabweans, or the Zulus.

He flicks ash to the wind.

– If you want carvings, that is another thing.

He jabs his fag towards me to underscore his teaching.

Curiously, for one who is neither black nor white, Zero loves to pigeonhole folk. *If you want masks you find a Gambian. If you want a sarong you find a Kenyan. If you want carvings you find a Tanzanian. If you want dope you find a Nigerian who will just happen to know a man who has carted his taboo cargo down from Lesotho's skylands, Sherpa style.*

Zimbabwean beadwork. (On wire. The Zulus do it on string.) That's the *trading goods* in the Johnnie Walker boxes: tangled, vivid menageries of animals and birds and fish.

– It'll be a breeze, Zero tunes. Tourists love this indigenous shit.

I would point out to him that the beadwork being Zimbabwean rather than South African renders it rather non-indigenous, but he'd just tune: *Selling shit is all about selling an illusion.* In Zero's eyes there is no objective truth.

– I hope so. I hope they go down well.

– Like selling grass to a hippie. Whatever you make over cost, you pocket. *Capito?* So haggle hard. Beat folk down.

Zero's Survival Tip #2. Haggle hard.

He hands me money for a second-hand Vespa he bid for after seeing an advert in the paper. I just need to pick it up from an old, glass-eyed priest who has not ridden the thing since he lost an eye in the township riots of 1976.

As Zero rides away in his empty Benz, he winds down to call offhandedly:

– Hey, Jero. I love you, my *laaitie*.

Then he's gone. I, his *laaitie*, his boy, feel stranded in the wake of his upbeat bravado. I'm cut off from all that's defined my life so far, other than a few books. And the tourist trinkets: Zero's jetsam.

A crow's wry *faawk* mocks my loneliness.

The light fades. I go to find this pizza joint.

4

Just south of the Limpopo River. After dusk.

The scattering of stars reminds Jabulani of fishing pontoons at night on Lake Kariba: the way they lure kapenta with a dazzling light.

He drops from the acacia to his feet and runs on in the loping stride of a distance runner.

He has always run. Run the long dusty miles to school as a boy. Run on the track at the university in Harare. Run at dusk for years to calm his mind after another day of teaching and marking papers.

He runs hour after hour in fear of a snake fanging him or a bullet felling him. And as he runs he recalls how he used to put his feet up for a pipe smoke after putting his son and daughter to bed. He'd let the cat doze on his lap and tune into Billie Holiday. It was at such times, as smoke floated up from his pipe through the overhanging fever tree to the Southern Cross, that he tallied up his good luck:

The magic of drifting into dreams as he lay in the dark against Thokozile's spine.

Tendai coolly hula-hooping at dusk under the papaya, hardly a hint of lackadaisical lilt in her hips. The way she drew butterflies and angels in fluid lines without lifting her pencil from paper. The way she saw him as her hero for carrying her high on his shoulders through the flaring bazaar, for catching moths and spiders in his bare hands, for reading to her in a range of voices.

Panganai finger-picking Bob Marley on his guitar in the hope of dazzling the girls who drifted by. The way he lost himself so deep in a novel he'd not feel mosquitoes stinging him or the cat rubbing her fur against the soles of his feet.

As Jabulani runs on through a dark savannah under a winking sliver of moon, he thinks: Bob Marley had held out such high hopes for this free Zimbabwe. And now Zimbabwe's gone to the dogs.

One time he has to sidestep a black cow shifting out of shadow.

A monkey-thorn draws a red thread across his forehead.

He hears shots in the distance. The farmers are out hunting.

The shots recall how, years ago, a band of renegade war veterans under a man they called Hitler had *yahooed* through his town in a pickup. They had shot their totemic AK-47s at an invulnerable sun, cut a blue sky to ribbons with their *panga* blades. They had flipped the corpse of a woman from the flatbed of that pickup. Her head had jounced rubberly in the dust. A breast had been *pangaed* off.

That image spurs him to run harder.

5

Hermanus. Before sunup.

A bird pecking at his refection yanks me out of a dream of the painting of the severed zebra's head that hangs over my folks' bed. In my dream a drop of paint fell from the canvas and landed on my mother's forehead to form a vermilion *bindi*. Then a gecko slid over her wan skin and sipped at the spot of blood. The sound of his echoing call was the sound of stones being tapped under water till it morphed into the sound of a beak pecking at glass.

I smack cold water over my face. I avoid the stranger in the mirror and look instead at my mother's watercolour of the seagull.

I gulp silty water from the tap.

This is the time she'd wordlessly put a cup of black coffee and yesterday's *Cape Times* next to my bed. She'd draw the curtain and slide the window up. She'd let her palm linger on my forehead, as if she feared a fever. She'd wordlessly pick up my concertinaed jeans from the floor and hang them over a chair. Through the window I'd hear turtle-doves singing their bobbing-headed Jewish chants, and the *muezzin* cajoling Malays to the mosque.

I yearn for the bitterness of my mother's coffee and for a gone boyhood of being sandy and sunburnt, of spicy samosas and sweet tea.

Now through this window I discern white foam sparking over dark rocks. The wind is cold and sea-tangy.

As I put on my Nikes and a fraying rugby jersey, I study the fantasy figures I have pencilled on the walls of my cell: mermaid angels, dog sharks, impala-headed girls, a sphinx. Figures borrowed from my mother's mind.

A few Xhosa girls line up with jerrycans and drums at a tap in a churchyard. They tap water for free. They giggle and gabble a scattering of *clicks* and *pips* like record needles snaring on scratches or grasshoppers snapping their wings in the air. They teasingly call *baleka baleka* after me and this puts vim into my step.

Waves crescendo against a heedless laager of rocks. I see a dead cormorant caught in a rock cleft. I free it and fling it out to sea where kelp bobs like seal heads in the surf. I imagine fish picking at the dead bird and crabs squabbling over the bones.

I follow the cliff path to the old harbour.

A hobo lies under a flipped-over fishing boat.

His bastard dog – half border, half other – tilts his head up and snarls his fangs at me.

The hobo's eyelids peel to reveal eyes red as raw sores. A milky tear travels along a deep crow's-foot in his windburnt skin. He murmurs to the dog.

The dog hides his teeth and wags his tail. I hold out my hand and he licks it.

The hobo oozes a weird wisdom from under the earflaps of his hunting hat, as if he's figured out the riddle of human pain. His bird-like face recalls Samuel Beckett.

– Your dog's beautiful. He or she?

– Bitch.

– Aha. She has beautiful fur.

– Skunk colours.

– Half border, hey?

– Any fool can tell.

– And boxer?

– Rhodesian.

– Aha. Had her long?

– How do you measure such a thing?

– Hey, I just wanted to say she's beautiful.

– How do you define *beautiful*?

– I'm sorry if I caught you in a sour mood.

– I'm not sour. You sidestep questions.

– Maybe we can shoot the breeze another time. I'll buy you a coffee. How does that sound?

He just snorts and turns his head away.

I stand spurned on the harbour wall. A seagull marks time over my head.

I run on along the path, following the shoreline, through a kind of limbo curiously devoid of all the caterwauling and mosque-calling of a Cape Town dawn. I run past the Marine Hotel, past Kwaai-water, past Voëlklip and all the way out to a long lagoon beach that reels out forever. The beach is empty. One lone sculler plies the lagoon. A luminous balloon of a sun tints the sea *perlemoen* pink.

At Voëlklip I stand on the rocks and scan a listlessly lilting sea for the telltale V of spray: a whale's blow. No luck. Just a distant fishing boat. And the sun tugs free of her low mooring and floats ropelessly.

I run on again. Just before I come to the tidal pool below the Marine Hotel, a hullabaloo of flocking seagulls draws my eyes to a sun-flared mirage on the path ahead.

Seagulls, flapping like ticker tape in a berg wind, fuss and flock over a sylphlike girl holding half a loaf of white bread in her hand.

My feet falter. The path pivots under me. Out at sea a southern right whale surfaces.

Bread. Girl of skin and hair and bone. She's no mirage.

The sun skips off seagull feathers like stray sparks. Cocky sparrows land whistling on her sun-haloed head. Ratty *dassies* gaze beady eyes at her, then dart for the bread she scatters at her bare feet. Her light white dress dances a flirting flamenco in the wind. Sunlight filters through the filmy cloth to hint at her sinuous figure.

Seeing me gawp lamely, she calms her dress with her hands. Then she laughs a string of pearls.

I gasp a draft of air. White noise hazes through my gaffed head.

She casts the last of the bread to the bickering gulls.

A gecko-fingered, sweet-smelling frangipani drops white petals as she walks into a low-walled yard. Hibiscus flares a lurid red. Cannas spit fames of yellow and orange. A sunbird blurs from aloe flower to aloe flower: a dizzying, unearthly green.

Hermanus is no longer a dim, far-flung town. It is the compass foot of a world shot in Fujifilm.

I run on. My feet dance like an impala's.

6

Somewhere south of the Limpopo.

At first Jabulani thinks the crow-dark shadow under a far acacia is a rock. Then it shifts in a way rocks don't.

His feet shuffle to a halt in the dust. He squints into the low, shimmering sun to figure it out.

He sees the telltale, inverted double V.

His instinctive, heart-jolting thought is *Hyena!*

But a hyena would have yipped his lust to the sky by now. This crouching animal eyes him coolly, biding his time.

Fear shoots through Jabulani's bones. Yet he stands dead still, casting his eyes about for stones.

No stones. Just wiry grass and dark dust.

He drops a shoulder to swing his rucksack free.

The animal unfolds again. The outline's too slick to be a ragged-skinned wild dog. It has to be a stray farm dog.

33

Jabulani fiddles his pocketknife out of his rucksack, then takes one slow step backwards.

The dog sniffs his brew of raw fear, smoky sweat and dry blood.

If he turns on his heels now, the dog will go for him. He has to hold his gaze. His life hangs on it.

The dog snarls his snaggle-toothed jaw at him.

Jabulani's plan is to hurl his rucksack skywards if the dog goes for him. The dog will shift focus to pivot his head after the decoy. Then Jabulani can sidestep and stab the dog in his neck.

If the dog's momentum plucks the knife from his hand, he'll just have to go for the eyes with his tatty All Stars.

Out of the corner of his eye, Jabulani sees another black form peel out of the dust. Another dog, he thinks.

Then another. And another. Four demon dogs homing in on him from four compass points.

Change of plan. He'll have to fight with the knife. Swing wildly, instead of stabbing deep.

He draws his tin canteen out of his rucksack and hurls it at Snaggletooth.

It jangles against his skull. He yelps and his feet jitter and jig.

The other dogs flick their eyes away from Jabulani for a moment to witness Snaggletooth stalking the canteen in the dust and sniffing at it. Then they focus on Jabulani again.

Now all four dogs inch towards him. Now he sees their viscous pink gums. Now the low rattling of their bloodlust sours his blood.

He wonders if his rucksack and passport would ever be found, if Thokozile would ever hear he'd died just south of the border.

A dog with a jagged, tooth-torn ear drops low. Instinct scripts this dog with the sun behind him to make the first move. He leaps at Jabulani.

Jabulani sidesteps and swipes wildly at the dog's head.

The dog spins away from him, yelping. Drops of blood from his lip fleck the dust. He paws at his bleeding lip. His yelping fades to a mystified whining. He shakes his head and blood fans out from him.

As in a kung fu film the others waver and glance at one another. They are no longer keen to go solo.

The bleeding dog falls in again, due east.

They drop their heads. They lay their ears flat. They no longer growl. It is this silence of unflinching communal focus that tells him this is the kill.

Flinging his rucksack might just off-foot one, and he might wound another with the knife, but two would still be free to gut him.

He begs God: *Keep an eye on my sweet-sweet Thokozile, on my soul-boy Panganai and my angel-girl Tendai.*

Then, out of the blue, they all tilt their heads in sync, as if to tune into rumours of blood on a high, inhuman frequency.

He sees distant dust float skyward.

The dogs figure they have no time to make the kill, yet find it hard to let their prey go.

Now he hears the motor throbbing deep.

And he sees sand spit up at their feet just before the shot cracks in his ears.

The dogs spin on their heels and lope away, tails tucked. Each time a shot is fired their asses flinch as if a whip tip has stung them.

A Land Rover painted in zebra markings jerks to a halt.

– Lucky bastard, a voice calls through a haze of dust.

As the dust fades he sees two white gunmen standing on the roof of the Land Rover, like tiger hunters riding high on a howdah.

The black man behind the wheel gazes pityingly at Jabulani.

7

Hermanus market.

The sky is a plane-chalked blue blackboard.

The sun treks doggedly through the blue, painting the surface of things below a kind of yellow. That sunlight in Amsterdam's too white and thin. This is viscous and chardonnayed.

The fuzzy radio-static zither of the sea echoes the thrum in my blood whenever I conjure her, the seagull girl.

The market echoes with the untuned, behind-the-scenes hubbub of shifting scaffolding, toppling boxes and jockeying vans. Smells waft by of jasmine joss, kelp, gas, dust, coffee, skinned oranges.

Long planks balance on two sawhorses under the tarp roof of my end-of-the-row stand. I lay out the bead things one by one: penguins, seahorses, chameleons, geckos, turtles, fish, sharks, dolphins, whales . . .

Next stall along, to my left, a wiry woman fiddles with her print-er's trays of stones and fossils.

I remember now that as a boy I dreamed of having an amber stone with a spider caught in it.

Next stall along again, a guy from Senegal sells vividly painted figures carved out of wood. They hold a myriad of jobs from teacher to soldier. I wonder how he'd depict a poet (pencil and paper in hand? scratching his head?). How he'd make him stand out from a philosopher or a clerk.

In this market no defined measure marks out the time. Trade will get under way once the first tourist moseys along to find a curio, or the first hotel keeper comes to finger fresh steenbrass or mango.

I see the fishing-boat hobo hobble across the cobbled square to the Fisherman's Cottage, his dog at his heels. The hobo's spine is curved as a scorpion's stinger under his ratty herringbone tweed. He hovers at the door to the pub till they give him a take-away cup of something. Maybe yesterday's coffee.

He slides his hooked spine down the bark of a fig tree just across the square from my stand. He squats on his heels in the sketchy shade and blows into the cup.

I nod his way and he stares through me, as if he's never seen me before.

His dog lies at his feet and idly surveys the chaos of the market moments before the theatre begins.

I sense the dog loves his hobo, has no sense his master is on so low a rung in the eyes of the world. But then a hawker's hardly higher than a hobo in any hierarchy.

– Never skips a day, the stoneseller chirps. He'll be under that fig till noon tying bits of flotsam string together. He was a professor of something or other at Rhodes University. Philosophy, I think. He and his wife came to Hermanus to watch the whales one September,

37

years ago. The whales were basking just off the rocks down by the old harbour. A fluke wave snatched his wife off the rocks. She died . . . and ever since then he's not gone further than a stone's throw from the sea.

– Did he tell you?

– It was in all the papers. And I saw it happen from up by the railing. I'd heard the yells and ran over from my stall. He'd gone in after her and folk yelled: *Swim out! Swim out!* But she was just too scared of the whales. It's against all human instinct to swim out towards them. And so the sea pounded her against the rocks till her head bled and she went down.

– That's hard.

– Yes. Another fella dived in and hauled the professor out. The professor fought tooth and nail. He wanted to go down with his wife. The fella had to hit him in the face.

I study the old professor's wind-lined face. He puts his coffee cup on his head and fiddles a few strands of string out of his pocket.

Then I put my hand out to the stone seller.

– Hey, I'm Jerusalem.

Her forehead furrows as she figures whether I'm dark white (maybe Italian?) or light coloured.

– Jerusalem Cupido.

Cupido. An incurably Cape Coloured name.

She bares sepia teeth through papery lips. Her dry skin scratches my palm.

– Hunter, she says.

– Hunter?

– Lily Hunter. But Lily sounds too sweet for a hardy old bird, hey?

– Hunter's cool.

– Jerusalem's exotic, she says. I never thought of it as a name for a boy.

I see in her bloodshot eyes a hint of fumbled coyness, as if recalling dusty lines from a school poem learned by rote.

– Well, I was born Jude, but no one ever calls me that. Jerusalem's my father's joke. You see, I'm half Muslim, half Jew. And the Muslim half of me is half Malay, half Cuban. My blood's a novel of journeys south from Malacca, Havana and Vienna.

– Sounds romantic. A taboo love between Muslim and Jew.

– Their love faded out long ago. If not for me, there'd be no proof of it.

– Tricky for your folks, I imagine . . . under apartheid.

– I was born in Amsterdam. If they'd stayed in South Africa they'd have been jailed. After Mandela got out it was no longer taboo.

– He's a god, hey?

– Mandela? *Ja*. A god.

– So, who do you bow to? Allah or Jehovah?

– Neither. I never found God in temple or synagogue.

Maybe God hides in the static between radio stations, in gaps between frames in film, in gullies between panels in comics, in silences between lines of a play. Or maybe God's found in the metamorphosis of things: the forming of a pearl around a speck of sand, the sea-honing of a sharp shard of beer glass into something smooth-rimmed and beautiful, in the journey of pressed grapes to wine, the paring down of a squid to the cuttlebone.

Zero Cupido never went to the temple again after he ran away from his folks at fourteen. To him the call of the *muezzin* is now just a distant mosquito whine in the soundtrack of a Cape dusk, along with the cries of newspaper boys and the crooning of pigeons.

I dimly recall an outing with my mother to a synagogue in a distant town (beyond the range of her shame). I sat-and-stood, sat-and-stood among men who murmured cricket scores, fiscal figures and horse tips while the rabbi intoned monotonously. I saw a fly wing into the gaping mouth of a snoring old man and I giggled until my mother scowled at me from the shadows.

– I lost my faith in God . . . long ago, Hunter sighs.

I sense that the thing that wiped out her faith is too deep and raw to reveal offhandedly.

At that moment the hobo's dog stalks a chip packet scudding across the cobbles. He traps it underfoot and licks the salt off.

– How does he survive, that dog?

– That dog? Moonfleet? Folk drop scraps as they go by.

– *Moonfleet.* Far out. Hey, by the way, do you have an amber with a spider caught in it?

– I have ants trapped in amber.

She rummages in a printer's tray, then puts a honey-yellow stone in my hands.

I hold it up to the sun. I squint at the filament of an ant fossil.

– How much is it?

– It's for a girl, isn't it?

I feel my cheeks colour at being caught out.

– Your girlfriend?

– No. Just a girl. I don't know her name yet.

– *Just a girl?* I see. I tell you what. I'll trade this for that turquoise whale. It'll perk up my old caravan no end. It'll pick up the colour of my everlastings.

I picture Hunter's lonely life in a caravan shared with mute stones and tacky dry flowers.

8

A farm somewhere south of the Limpopo.

Two Dobermann dogs come walloping and hollering out of a zinc-roofed farmhouse. Claws scuttling over stones, tails whipping wildly.

A peacock flies up into a giant bluegum, calling *kaaaaow, kaaaaow*.

The gunmen yell at the dogs.

The cowed dogs sniff at Jabulani's feet.

Behind the farmhouse is a long row of barns, like marooned boxcars on a desert siding.

Followed by yapping dogs, the gunmen frogmarch Jabulani past a fenced-in pond where crocodiles V their jaws to stay cool. They blind-eye white chickens dangling dead from a wire.

– Ever since they taste Zimbos they gone off chicken, jokes the one with a scar slanting south-east from his left eye.

His sidekick laughs.

A door slides on rails. Jabulani is flung to the sawdust-covered floor. He hears the wounded call of the peacock over the yapping of the dogs. He smells smoke and the snuff of dry tobacco. As his eyes focus in the slats of slanting light, he sees he's not alone. An old black man is stirring a smoking pot of *pap* cooking over a fire drum. The furrowed vellum of his forehead is caught in a shaft of dust-dancing sun.

Jabulani imagines he'll see tobacco hanging bat-like overhead. Instead, a bare beam runs from one end of the barn to the other. Steel bunk beds line the walls. Grey jail blankets with footnote white lines are folded into squares.

An old, sagging-skinned bloodhound lifts raw eyes out of a concertinaed jowl to peer at the stranger.

– Where am I?

– This is hell. You'll wish you never crossed over.

– Hell?

– We're slaves, man. You, me . . . the others out on the lands.

– Others?

– The other fugitives they caught.

– But they can't just round up men like cattle.

– When they have the guns they can do what they want. There's no higher law out here.

The old dog farts, as if to underscore his words.

The old man spoons some *pap* into an enamel bowl and hands it to Jabulani.

– I am too old to dig holes, so I cook.

Jabulani forms the *pap* into a ball in his fist and wolfs it down.

– It's good.

The old man nods. He scoops water from a deep drum into an enamel yellow mug from a long row of such mugs hanging on nails. This too he hands to Jabulani.

Jabulani swigs the cool, sweet water in gasping gulps, washing the *pap* down.

– Your dog is old, notes Jabulani.

– They wanted to shoot him. Half his teeth have gone. They taught him to hunt down fugitives. To hunt you and me.

The old man offers his hand to the dog and laughs as the dog licks it.

– Some hunter, hey?

Jabulani laughs. It feels good to laugh after the river and the dogs and the gunmen.

– You too will be sent to dig holes this afternoon.

– Holes?

– For the poles for the camo shade cloth they span over the marijuana. So you can't see it from the sky and so the marijuana does not die.

– They farm marijuana?

– Now you farm marijuana. They will put you in a crew called Polemen. The Polemen are the rebels and newcomers . . . the ones who cannot hide the fire in their eyes. They stay Polemen till their heads hang, until their spines hook and their feet drag. Then they become zombies. We call the zombies Shadowmen. They have given up all hope of escape. They travel in a truck to the Limpopo before sunup and fill drums with water for the marijuana. They spend the day in the shadows of the shade cloths. They plant the young marijuana four feet apart and water it just a bit each day. Not too much, otherwise the roots rot. And they pick the tops to dry out for *ganja*.

– How long have you been on this farm?

– Two and a half years. My wife has heard no word from me since I came to South Africa. I was a baker in Harare.

– Is there no way to escape? To send word out to the world?

– They who run get shot down like old dogs. The vultures pick their bones. I once sent word on a paper tied to the foot of a pigeon that landed on this barn. He had lost his bearings for a time. He had a ringed foot, so chances are good my paper was read somewhere. The catch is, whoever read it would think the words were the scribblings of a madman. Besides, I cannot map out where we are. There are no landmarks in this dry borderland.

Jabulani gauges from the distance he ran and the pickup ride that they must be about a marathon's distance from the border.

The old man puts out his empty hand.

– I am Jonas.

– I am Jabulani.

They shake, palm to palm, then swivel their hands to hook their thumbs.

9

Hermanus market.

Vans have unloaded their cargo. Cardboard boxes have spilt their wares. I have put out my beaded animals.

The market is a jamboree of colours: Kenyan cotton sarongs called *kikois*, bolts of Indian cloth, Chinese silks, pyramids of mangos and oranges, yellow and red peppers, and golden bananas.

The market echoes with the rapping of the Tanzanians hawking their wood carvings, the muttering of a faux Zulu shaman fogging magic *muti* (a mix of beetroot, garlic and honey) to cure you of The Virus and still another hex in a vial to spook snakes away, the keening of a Moroccan snake-charmer's flute, the dry-bone music of marimba men from Malawi and the haunting howl of the whale crier's kelp horn.

Instead of riding listing, laden boats to Spain or Italy, young

Africans with a fiery dream may head south, leaving behind them countries where a leopard-hatted ruler fattens his gut on overseas funds. They spend all their money on rides under tarps in trucks, in the holds of cargo boats. Or they walk for miles and miles, crossing borders, dodging the men and animals that prey on them under a vulture-zoned sky. By hook or by crook they find their way south to Cape Town, the London of Africa. And further south still to this marketplace.

A villagey, matey vibe pervades the market. Traders whistle or wave across the square; they shake hands and linger.

Now locals and holidaymakers drift into the square. You can tell them apart. The locals have sun-jaded, wind-scratched skin and a lazy lilt to their walk. They have lost their stiffness. The slick holidaymakers from Johannesburg up north tend to have an upbeat skip to their walk. They strive to look chilled in their Billabong gear and flip-flops, but they stay tuned to their cellphones in case a deal eludes them. The pale-skinned holidaymakers from overseas stand out like folk from another planet with their muted joy, Crumpler bags and colourful Crocs.

A coloured fruit seller pitches his high call over this jumble of voices. *Liii-tchiii. Liii-tchiii.*

Seeing me tuned in, he lobs a red ball to me across the square. I dart to catch it.

The spiky skin stings my palm. I pop the reptilian peel between my teeth and suck the slick sweet off the stone.

– Who's stall's this?! a bass voice booms.

I spin to see a fat ass forming big bongos in front of my stall.

The video-toting tourist in hard-core hiking boots flips over the bead animals as if to find some flaw in the handiwork. She spurns them one by one: topples a giraffe, tips a turtle's feet up, tangles gecko tails.

– How much?

I hope to stay calm as I put the animals on their feet again.

– Depends. Was there one you had in mind?

She picks up a penguin.

– How much for this here bird? she twangs.

– That penguin's a hundred rand.

– One hundred? I'll give you half.

She plonks the penguin down and manhandles a gecko instead. So far I've traded a whale for a stone and now a woman wants a penguin at cost. I have *nada* to hand over to Zero, never mind profit to pocket. I ought to heed Zero's Survival Tip #2 and haggle to and fro, but her gung-ho air kills this tango.

– I'm sorry. That's what I want for it.

– You just lost money, boy.

She drops the gecko and shunts on to Hunter's cowries.

– You walk on by, shoots Hunter. I have fuckall to sell to you.

The woman stomps off, lugging binoculars and bazooka-lensed camera.

Hunter laughs and I echo her as I fix the penguin's bent feet.

Hunter and me in cahoots. An old white woman with dry, gooseberry-husk skin and a lovesick coloured boy. A killer duo.

A whisper of paper swirls over the hard fabric of the world.

I can smell low-tide kelp on the cool harbour wind.

I realise I haven't seen the stray market dogs all day.

10

A farm somewhere south of the Limpopo. Noon.

Panganai and Tendai tug tufts of candyfloss from pink clouds as the Chinese girl in a pink tutu rides a circus horse round and round.

The frenzied jabber of the dogs and the rumble of a diesel pickup haul Jabulani out of reverie.

He smells the *pap* Jonas has cooked in the dusty, dour light.

A yelled command is a high note over the deep-river tones of men singing in his language.

Jabulani gears himself to see a gang of hardened, jaded old men.

The barn door slides open and the men plod in. They give off a gamey reek of smoke and sweat.

Sidestepping the stranger, they scoop water out of the drum with enamel mugs. They drink half and tip half over their heads. The curing cool of the water draws smiles from a few of the men.

Jonas shyly shuffles his feet. The men are younger and jauntier than he had imagined. They must be Polemen.

– Boys, this is Jabulani, says Jonas. He is a teacher.

The way they nod their sodden heads at him reveals deep awe of teachers. They all, not so long ago, sat at the feet of a teacher with a slate and chalk in hand, keen to learn about the world beyond the Limpopo.

Jabulani hops on to an old army troop truck with the Polemen.

The Polemen murmur their feeling of injustice as they go by the Shadowmen behind barbed wire. *They have it good. They stay under the shade cloths. They are not stung by the sun. They are not hounded by the gunmen.*

The marijuana the forlorn Shadowmen tend to under the shade cloths is absurdly green. A fizzing, green-mamba green. The plants dance as innocently as lotus or palm in the dry wind.

When the army truck halts on a dusty unwired space, they carry the poles from the back of the truck to put in the holes.

One of the men shinnies up a pole, hammer in his back pocket and nails in his mouth like some fanged demon gecko. They tie the shade cloth to a rope and he hauls it up and over the cross-beam. Once this is spun taut as trampoline skin he hammers it down.

Jabulani's job, just as Jonas forecast, is to dig holes with a pick.

All picks fall in sync. Men sing to the rhythm of the falling picks as red dust smokes skywards. If a man stands to rub his sore spine, a gunman barks at him to get on with the job.

A haggard, wiry man floating long, white, jute-like hair from under a cowboy hat rides a volatile horse to and fro.

He reminds Jabulani of old Willie Nelson: spiny white stubble, buzzardy eyes. He fleetingly recalls cold amber beers in a student dive in Harare, tuned into Nelson and Dylan.

Scarface and Sidekick dangle their army boots from the bonnet of the Land Rover.

Another two gunmen stand smoking in the shade of the troop truck.

Jabulani surveys the barren land around him. No chance of running without being gunned down.

A whip cracks. Jabulani jumps.

– Hey! This is not the beach. Dig or you'll feel the bite of my mamba.

The cowboy snarls his teeth into a gleeful sneer at the sight of the tenderfoot swinging his pick with gusto.

– That albino's the devil, a Poleman whispers to Jabulani. We call him Ghost Cowboy.

11

Hermanus market. Afternoon.

I catch sight of the seagull girl feeling and smelling oranges. My scalp tingles. My heart beats a snare-drum riff.

The fruit seller drops his chant to gawp at her. He skins a litchi with otter fingers and hands her the white ball.

From this angle I can't see her put it in her mouth.

He holds out a hand, palm up, for the stone.

I abandon my stall to see.

She bows to spit the stone into his hand.

He pockets it. Then he peels an orange and gives her a quarter.

I imagine juice seeping from her lips, for she wipes her chin with the heel of her hand. She nods at him.

He is over the moon. Winking theatrically, he fingers oranges as if fondling breasts. Cocky swine.

She laughs at his antics and signals she'll have half a dozen. A hand and a thumb.

He twists the paper bag as he hands it to her.

She drifts from stand to stand. Now she frivolously puts a sun hat on her head and tilts her head to see herself in a mirror. Now she stands to look at a guy in dangling dreads lazily juggling sticks. They are the things they call devil sticks, bound in rubber from bicycle tyres. Her eyes shake the dreadlock dude out of his torpid daze and now he makes his sticks sky-dance. She laughs at his dreads writhing like spiked snakes.

I pick up my guitar and sing Dylan in a bid to lure her away from him.

She heads my way, swinging her paper bag of oranges.

My heart beats hard.

Behind her, the jilted dreadlock dude catches his sticks and skims his hand off his ass at me for cutting in on his act.

Now the seagull girl stands in front of me. Her toenails are painted blue.

My voice drops out of key. I glance at Hunter, who reads all in a moment and frowns at me to focus.

– You play beautifully.

The girl's voice is limpid as the sound of a penny whistle, fresh as lemongrass, sweet as acacia honey.

I lay down my guitar. The uncut strings beyond the keys quiver like moth feelers.

She lets her fingers fondle the wire-and-bead animals. Each animal pulses to life under her fingertips. A penguin wags its stubby tail. A chameleon unfurls its fizzy tongue. A turtle tilts its head. She lifts a seahorse to the sky. Sunlight glints in the beads. The spine fin blurs like a hummingbird's wings. And as her fingers glide on, the animals freeze again.

I no longer see them as mere trinkets to hawk for Zero but as things with soul.

– How much do you want for this seahorse?

No words flow from my lips.

– They go for a hundred, Hunter pipes up. But maybe you could deal him down just a tad.

I scowl at Hunter.

– You can have him, I tell the seagull girl.

– That's sweet. But a hundred's a song for something so magical.

Before handing me the note, she folds it twice over, as if to render the deal less mercenary. Or as if to hand me a pencilled note.

As she goes past the fig tree, she drops an orange in the hobo's hands and bends to pat his dog.

I am dazed beyond all cure.

– You can't just give your wares away, Hunter scolds me.

– Isn't she a goddess?

– See her float, Hunter mocks. Catch her before she kites off.

Then her voice goes all minor key:

– I was beautiful once.

My eyes slide away.

I see a young black man running across the market square as if the devil is after him. He trips and falls hard at the feet of the seagull girl. His mouth gapes, as if to tell her something. Maybe to beg her to pluck out the knife sticking into his spine. Instead, he spits blood on her sandalled feet.

The bag of oranges falls. The bag splits and oranges scatter. There's an eerie hiatus before her voice skirls over the market.

The dreadlock dude's devil sticks fall.

The fruit seller abandons his chant between syllables. *Liii . . .*

I feel as if I am running underwater, through kelp. I can hardly swing my feet.

The hobo professor catches her as she falls. He lays her head down in the green-tinted shade of his fig tree. Her hair spills like that of Venus coming out of the sea. Moonfleet sniffs at her.

I tug off my T-shirt and slide it under her head.

A man comes out of the Fisherman's Cottage with a glass in hand.

I beg him for the glass. I tip out the liquid and lemon rind and catch a cube of ice in my hand. I slide ice over her forehead and along her arms. By now we are surrounded by a throng of gazers who frown at my zany method. Once the ice melts, my fingers ghost over her skin.

In my mind her skin's a flawless canvas. I paint in pale-pink nipples and her navel, a comma halving the flat plane between the parentheses of her hips.

The bleeding man writhes wordlessly. His head is pooled in blood.

How can I conjure fantasies of a girl while a man's life bleeds away? How come folk all tune in to her fate rather than his?

Only now the man from the Fisherman's Cottage goes to call an ambulance.

And the dreadlock dude tugs the knife out. Then he stabs it into the fig tree and wipes his hands on his jeans.

And the hobo has a shot at plugging the wound with his hands.

I feel a ripple under the seagull girl's skin. Her eyelids flicker and lift subtly and her eyes glint through narrow slits before her lids fall again. Then, suddenly, her eyelids peel apart to reveal her lagoon-green eyes. I smile at her but she stares through me. I want to kiss the hint of squint lines fanning out from the corner of her eyes, or the cinnamon stipples along her cheekbones.

Now other folk cart her away to the Burgundy Hotel. I feel as if they want to pluck her white skin away from my coloured hands.

Now the man's dead and the stabbed fig tree weeps white sap and the hobo's hands are stained red.

I pick up my T-shirt. I find a thread of her hair, virile as horse-hair. I fiddle it round a finger and hold it up to the sun. Then I cover the head of the dead man with my T-shirt.

Around me folk voice their verdict on the murder. How this is proof of a country going to the dogs. How he must have done something dodgy.

The professor rifles through the man's pockets and finds a tatty, warped passport.

– He's from Zim.

– Just another refugee, says the fruit seller.

Moonfleet laps at the pool of clotting blood.

– We are all refugees in this land, tunes the professor to his dog.

Then he clicks bloody fingers and they go: the professor's earflaps flapping, a tatty string dangling from his pocket, Moonfleet's tail til-lering through the wind.

A siren yowls at an impervious sun.

At my stall again, I hide the seagull girl's hair in a book: *Of Love and Other Demons.*

I put on my rugby jersey (always on hand for when the wind picks up).

– This town's not just whales and hibiscus, Hunter remarks. Things can get hazardous.

I forget my luck in finding a memento of her and slide into sor-row for this land where a man is killed for the sin of being foreign.

12

A farm somewhere south of the Limpopo. Dusk.

A hare hops across the veld and the gunmen drop their guns to trap it.

Ghost Cowboy slides from his saddle to join in the sport.

Each time the hare darts for a gap they flap scarecrow hands.

Ghost Cowboy flings a stone. The hare flinches as the stone *thups* into fur-hidden bone.

The men laugh.

Out of the corner of his eye Jabulani sees a Poleman run. His eyes pan to follow him. Behind him he hears the *haw-hawing* of the men and the dull tattoo of stones finding their mark.

He turns to see blood seeping through quivering fur.

Ghost Cowboy catches sight of the fleeing man and vaults onto his horse.

Ghost Cowboy fells him with one shot from his long gun.

The Zimbabwean cartwheels in the dust.

The horse's front hooves dance around the baying head of the fallen man. The horseman coolly fires another shot from the saddle. The man's head jerks before the bullet whiplashes in Jabulani's ears.

The horseman nooses the man's foot and tows him through the dust.

The gunmen order the Polemen to fling him onto the back of the Land Rover. For the crocodiles.

Then the Polemen sing again to the rhythm of the falling picks. They are not yet dead, so they sing. They sing of the sight of their village when they journey home by train after a long exile. They sing of the healing, humid balm of a woman's hips. They sing of the magic in the dancing feet of a young girl.

Far to the north, across the Limpopo, a woman senses her man died a dry, bitter death and a wail pipes from her lips to the sun.

13

Hermanus. Another sunup.

Seagulls mewl and loop in a mother-of-pearl sky. Sparrows chirrup cheerily in the frangipani. *Dassies* drift out of hiding.

The seagull girl comes out of the white house, bread in hand.

Sparrows take flight as she floats towards the frangipani.

She comes to a standstill, bamboozled by this wonder. The frangipani's fingers bear a myriad of vivid oranges.

I stay hiding in the *fynbos*. I laugh in my soul at the sight of her rubbing her eyes.

She picks one of the oranges and handles it as if to prove it is not dreamt. She tosses the orange up and catches it, tosses it up and catches it.

I hear the sweet smack of the rind in her palm. She looks at me without seeing me.

As she comes out of the gate, she drops the orange into a pocket of her dress.

She flings bread to the gulls and *dassies*, then holds out a hand for the sparrows to peck from. All the while she casts her eyes about in the hope of unravelling the enigma of the frangipani.

When the bread is all gone she walks down the stone steps to the tidal pool.

At the edge of the pool she peels down to a jade bikini. Tattooed angel wings arc from her shoulder blades to flirt with the hem of her low-slung bikini. The tenuous string of her bikini top stops her wings from unfurling to fly her, a girl Icarus, away over the blind blue deep of Walker Bay.

I flinch at the thought of the tattoo needle sliding its black blood under her skin.

She dives headlong into the pool. The water warps her outline, forming sine-wave contours as she glides under the surface. She comes up gasping from the cold. Then she swims butterfly out to the far wall. With each forward swing of her arms, her wings slope up out of the water. I suck in a gasp of sea air at each sighting of her wings.

A high rogue wave sends fizzing foam over the wall, now to hide her from my eyes, now to reveal again her sinuous curves as the fizz fades. At the wall she does an oh-so-tidy flip turn, heels tucked to her sweet jade ass.

I feel faint.

Now she floats on the surface, fanning her toes to the sky the way hollow-boned old men do on the Dead Sea. She yields to the whim of ebb and fetch, and each time I fear she'll be sucked out to sea by an ebbing wave, another wave sweeps over the wall.

On this edge of the tidal pool it is merely the slight heft of an orange that keeps the wind from filching her flimsy dress.

*   *   *

I run on past the tidal pool, out to the flat, hard sand by the lagoon. I duck when a screaming gull dives down at me from the sky. It circles, then swoops again. This time its webbed claws graze my hands as I hood my scalp. I dart away from the dunes where the gull's eggs huddle in some hidden hollow.

14

A farm somewhere south of the Limpopo. Dusk.

They play football on hard, foot-mortared sand behind the farmhouse. The ball is shot far beyond the rickety posts.

Jabulani follows the ball into the *bundu* and a shot sings past his ear. He flings himself down in the dust.

The other Zimbabweans laugh. They have all had their turn to piss their pants for fetching a stray ball without a nod from the gunmen.

The gunmen put two crates of cold beer down. Before long the upbeat banter of the Zimbabweans is about football and girls. None allude to their shot countryman. None glance at the crocodile pond for fear of sighting a bone or foot.

The cold glass is soothing in Jabulani's skinned palms.

Beyond him he hears the yelps of the children of the gunmen

cavorting in the swimming pool. He craves the thought of gliding underwater as he used to in the school pool on weekends. He hears the rhythmic *dup dup* of a tennis ball on a tennis court. The sound recalls the *thupping* of stone into hare hide.

A peacock cries *caaaoooow*.

Jonas swings a *panga* blade down. A watermelon falls into gaping red hemispheres. He deftly slices it up.

The men flaunt absurd green Picasso grins as they gnaw at the watermelon rind.

A black girl carries a crate of beer to the gunmen. She wears no shirt. She is young.

The gunmen smirk at her bobbling breasts as she twists the lids off the beer bottles. Scarface pinches her ass.

Ghost Cowboy signals to Jabulani to come over.

He jogs up to the gunmen and the girl.

– Yes?

– Yes, master, Ghost Cowboy snarls.

– Yes, master.

– Do you find this girl pretty?

– She is pretty.

– Master.

– Master.

– Would you fuck her? baits Scarface.

– She's just a girl.

Ghost Cowboy squeezes a breast in his hand till she flinches from pain.

– She's ripe as a mango, tunes Ghost Cowboy.

– You are not a good man, master.

All the other white men guffaw.

– *Woooah*. You gonna go to hell, hey? Hey, hey? taunts Scarface.

– Will I go to hell, boy? Ghost Cowboy asks.

– That is for God to judge, Jabulani murmurs.

– God? If I make this girl go down on me now, will God be a hero? Will he shoot me down with a bolt? Or maybe send an angel to kill me dead? Remember how the Nazis turned Jew-skin into lampshades and God did fuckall. If not for the Americans they'd have wiped the Jews off the planet. Now Mugabe fucks you folk over and over again and the Americans look away this time. Then, *wahaaaaaa*, like some crazy jack-in-the-box God pitches up to judge *me*.

Jabulani hangs his head.

– I shot a man yesterday. You saw it, boy. I feel zero regret. No guilt. No fear of God. Check out my hand.

He holds his hand out flat, level with the earth.

– Still as a goddamn cadaver. Hey?

– Still, master.

– Now, tell me, why don't I shoot you? Just for the hell of it.

He forms a fist.

– I hold your life in my hand, boy.

– I have a wife and children. All I want is a job. I need to send money to them. If you let me go, master, I will walk away and forget I ever saw this place.

He unfurls his fist to wag a finger at Jabulani.

– But the thing is . . . the thing is, you can't forget my face.

The other gunmen laugh jadedly and spit in the dust.

– Tell you what I do. I let you job on this farm. I let you live. I give you beer. So maybe for you there is a God. Now, I think you've been rude to this girl. She has beautiful tits and yet you look down at your feet.

Jabulani shuffles his feet.

– Look at her.

Jabulani tilts his head up. He feels his *isinjonjo* go hard and shifts his hands to hide it.

– Your cock can't lie. You want her. Now I want you to go down on all fours and howl for her. Howl like a dog at the moon.

Jabulani glances at the other Zimbabweans. They all have their eyes on him. Jonas nods at him.

Jabulani goes down and lets out a wavering, wistful yelp.

Scarface kicks him in the ribs.

Now Jabulani, teacher of Orwell and Achebe, howls his pain, his fury, his sorry lust in this godless dust.

15

Hermanus. Dusk.

I mosey along through the emptying market square. I realise I have not penned a poem in a long time. It's as if the world, however vivid, swims and sways before me too elusively to pin down on paper: telegraph lines shiver like guitar strings, the sea swings, seagulls hem and haw, the earth quivers all day under the sun. Yet each line I put down feels flat, stale, stalled.

Men of all colours huddle round a motorcar radio to tune in to the cricket. An English wicket falls and they dance and high-five and sing out *HOWZAAAT!* In this country we rob, shoot and burn each other . . . until a cricket ball or rugby ball or football sends us into a shindig of sudden camaraderie and hooting and *vuvuzela* tooting.

After the high of beating the West Indies last Christmas, South Africa has had a jinxed year. We lost to Sri Lanka and India.

I catch sight of her at a pub table on the front deck of the Burgundy. Somehow I sense the guy she's with is her lover.

The umbrellas flap and jig in the wind as if they too are following the cricket. They feel zero empathy for my sudden sorrow.

I sit at a free table next to theirs. I wonder if she'll recognise me from the market, but she's scrutinising the tea bag floating in her china teacup.

HE: Hey, Lotte. You just happened to be there.

Lo-tte. A ballooning gasp of longing tied off with the tip of his tongue.

She fishes the tea bag out of her cup and pinches it unflinchingly between two fingers.

SHE: I felt he wanted to tell me something.

HE: But that's absurd.

SHE: I was the last thing he saw.

She shifts her teacup from palm to palm. Her gaze flickers over me.

HE: Focus now, Lotte.

He catches her hands in his.

HE: Come to Jozi with me.

Jozi, Johannesburg. Jazzy yet risky. A hip war-zone.

SHE: I won't be caged behind a razor-wired wall. Besides, I can't paint in Jozi.

She draws her hands away and *clinks* the teacup down on the saucer.

SHE: I need the sea.

He farts air through his pressed lips. Evidently he scorns the whims of artists who hang on such ethereal things as muses and vibe.

HE: Look . . . I want you to lie low till the weekend. Till I come again.

SHE: Lie low?

HE: Yesterday you had a foreigner's blood on your feet. Today some psycho fucked with your frangipani. I'm not superstitious . . . but perhaps they are signs.

SHE: I thought it was magic.

I grin like a dork.

HE: *Magic?* Black magic, maybe. If you stay I forbid you to walk alone along the sea path beyond Kwaaiwater, or to swim in the tidal pool at the crack of dawn.

SHE: Al, I love that path. I love to walk all the way to the lagoon. And I love the pool then. If you weren't always so wiped out we'd swim together.

Al. Maybe she's drawn to guys with curt names. She'll be spooked by my litany of vowels.

HE: It's not forever. Once I've done the paperwork for this Taiwan deal, things will plateau out. I can handle things from this end then. We'll marry and have a baby . . .

Under my feet: pebbles, a wine cork, bottle tops, cigarette ends, an oyster shell.

SHE: A girl.

HE: We'll tie her hair in pigtails.

SHE: We'll let her hair fall free.

HE: We'll dress her in jeans so she can skip and climb like a boy.

SHE: She'll wear a dress she tucks into her panties when she skips. And she won't care if boys see her panties when she's climbing. You want to curb her freedom when she's not even born yet. And you'll tell me I have to hide my breasts under a cloth if I nurse her in a café. You sound Muslim. Or American.

He just sulks for pity.

Lotte sends me a flicker of a smile, fleeting and ephemeral. Perhaps I imagined it. She spills sugar on the table and draws her finger through it. She frowns to figure out where she's seen me before.

A cockroach feather-foots over my foot to zero in on the sugar. I shudder.

Twin boys stand in front of the restaurant deck. They bow. One boy plays a tune on a Zulu hosepipe flute, and then words from Papageno's aria fly from the mouth of the other boy, words like dipping, flitting birds eluding the bird catcher.

Al tosses all the jingling small change from his pockets into their hat.

I fid a coin in my pocket.

They bow again and go into the orange light.

HE: Come to Jozi with me, Lotte. I beg of you.

I free my guitar and pluck the strings.

Lotte remembers now. She smiles at me and blows the sugar away.

I twang my desire for her.

Al slurps spilt liquid from his saucer.

SHE (laughing): Remind me why I love you, Al Pike.

HE: Because you need never be scared when I'm with you. And you'll never go begging. Besides, I swept you off your feet, didn't I?

SHE: You did?

HE: I did. And I gave you a flashy rock. See it catch the sun.

He holds her hand and swivels her ring so the diamond flashes like a lit fuse.

HE: You belong to me.

My plucking fades out.

SHE: Do I?

HE: You do.

They kiss.

I pinch a ten-rand note under my coffee cup.

A Tuareg four-by-four hoots at me as I jaywalk to the cliff path. I go down the steps to the old harbour. On the way down I pick red canna flowers. I fling the petals into the water of the harbour and see them float to form a question mark.

Is there no cure for this fever in my blood?

I sit on the harbour wall and play my guitar hard. The waves of a listless sea clap dully against the wall.

Seagulls mock me from the rickety salting poles where fishermen hang fish out to dry.

– Isn't she beautiful? I cry.

Kaaaak kaaaak is all they reply.

A few moth-eaten, sun-seeking *dassies* blink sorrowful eyes at me from the red zinc roof of the old whaling warehouse.

The professor, shadowed by Moonfleet, drifts down to the slanting slipway where whalers once landed harpooned whales.

Moonfleet skips and barks at my music. Seagulls fly from the salting poles. *Dassies* shy from the hot tin roof.

The professor rolls up his pants and wades barefoot in the shallows. His hands *t'ai chi* at the sky.

Moonfleet, all skipped out, licks the salt off the soles of my feet.

I play my guitar till my fingers bleed and the sun sinks west of the new harbour. And then I play on into the dusk, a fish bone for a fat pick.

16

A farm somewhere south of the Limpopo. After midnight.
Jonas picks Jabulani. There are muted murmurs of an injustice, for Jabulani has not had to endure this hell for long.

– Jabulani is the one who can run like a wild dog. Our forefathers were warriors and knew how to throw a spear, but that skill too is lost. Jabulani is the one who learnt at his university how to throw a javelin far. And if he survives, the police may listen to him, for he is a teacher.

They cast a rope over a beam, then tie it around Jabulani's hips. They hoist him up to the beam.

He signals for them to let go. He winds up the rope, looping it between thumb and elbow. He slings it over his collarbone.

Now they chuck the long, glowing-tipped stick up to him.

He catches it. Holding the stick ahead of him like a tightrope walker, he foot-foots along the beam, heel to toe, heel to toe.

They gasp and hiss each time he teeters. At the end of the beam he tilts a vent and hauls himself out onto the roof. Through the vent he hears a hum of hope from the condemned men.

He geckos up the roof slope to the zenith. The stars look like holes punched in Jonas's fire drum. Down below he sees the dogs lying flat, feet flirting with the glowing coals of a dying fire.

He stands and feels the heft of the stick in his hand. His target is over forty yards away. If the stick falls short, they will all suffer. Ghost Cowboy will kill him.

He hurls the stick at the thatched roof of the poolside gazebo. A dog barks at the whistle of this one-eyed sky snake spearing through the dark.

Soon the thatch begins to glow. A flame peels away. Then another. Then the gazebo roof is ablaze.

Now all the dogs go ape.

Jabulani drops flat to the roof.

The gunmen bound out of the farmhouse all bootless and cussing and eyes agog at the sparks shooting high.

A peacock flaps up towards the stars, tail feathers on fire.

The gunmen let the Zimbabweans out of the tobacco barn and yell at them to form a line from the pool to the farmhouse. No chance of saving the gazebo. They focus on dousing the farmhouse thatch before the flying sparks can catch.

Jabulani sees slopping buckets jig from hand to hand. He sees the flaming peacock fall out of the sky: a phoenix scattering firework feathers.

He slides down the far slope of the roof and jumps.

Then he runs hard along the rutted dirt road.

A porcupine darts across his path, rattling his quills like a shaman shaking bones and shells.

After maybe two miles, he comes out onto the tarred road, where he finds south by the stars and runs again.

Lost in this bushman rhythm, he hears the screams of the flaming peacock looping again and again through his head.

He hears the sound of a motor and turns to peer into blinding headlights. He fears it may be from the farm but it is not the low throb of a Landy. Gambling on it being a stranger, he holds out his thumb.

The headlights polaroid the skull of an ox spiked on a pole. He saves this image in his mind.

A woman alone in a Pajero. She winds down the window. Nina Simone's voice floats out, mingling with smoke from a jay held in peace-sign fingers.

– Where you heading?

– Cape Town.

– You dig Nina?

– Huh?

– Do you love Nina Simone?

– I love her.

– Well, hop in then.

She hands the glowing joint to him.

He sucks deep and long.

– There's an icebox at your feet.

He cracks a can of Windhoek Lager.

They ride the wake of flaring headlights through an indigo universe. For a long time no words mar the giddy high of escape.

The grass and beer put him in a forward, flirty frame of mind.

– I thought lone white women never pick up black men.

– It's crazy. I ought to be *manhandled*.

She laughs, winds down the window to fillip out the butt of the jay.

He sees deep down her zaftig bosom.

– But this Marley magic fucks with your head, hey? she shouts over the whine of the wind.

– It does rather.

She winds up the window.

– You from Zim?

– I am.

– I thought so. You looked shit scared. The proverbial rabbit in the headlights.

Now he laughs at this pigeonholing of Zimbabweans. It feels good to laugh. He has not laughed freely since his life began to unravel half a year ago.

Nina's voice is a viscous, velvety red wine.

– Mates of yours?

Headlights fare in the rearview. He swivels his head and squints into the glare. The safari Land Rover bullets into focus. Ghost Cowboy rides shotgun. His long white hair flames in the wind as he draws a bead on the Pajero with his long gun.

– If we survive, I want you to fuck me. Deal?

A shot zings over the roof of the Pajero.

Jabulani instinctively ducks. He senses this isn't the moment to tell her he hasn't yet been unfaithful to Thokozile.

– Tell me your name.

– Call me Nina, for now. Yours?

– Freedom.

He always tells white folk his white name. They want a pithy Western handle to call you by, rather than your African name.

– Freedom? Cool! So you and me, Freedom, we find a motel, yeah?

73

In the rearview Jabulani sees the gun spark just before the rear window implodes.

– Yeah?

– Yeah.

She foots the gas hard and the Pajero shoots ahead. Zoned on marijuana and the thrill of outfooting the hunter, she yips at the gecko moon.

The beams of the Pajero fall south like dying shooting stars.

At dawn they are far south of Johannesburg, that hard, hazardous city of gold-seekers that they'd skirted in the dark. And now the N1 cuts an unflinching blue line down to Cape Town.

A lone woman carting boxes and a pot on top of her turban surfaces out of the dancing haze on the tar. She dangles a live chicken swinging beak-down from her hand.

And further on a cart made from the plundered corpse of an old pickup follows on the heels of a sagging, dusty donkey.

And yet further still an old rag-and-bone woman hawks sunflowers from under a faded beach umbrella.

A boy flutters his hands as if swimming in the liquid mirage. His hands draw their eyes to his windmills crafted from wire, cans and dead time.

Jabulani recalls his boyhood of fishing in the river and killing birds and lizards and sucking udder-hot milk out of his hands and learning the art of stick fighting. He recalls walking for miles down a dust track to a tar road where he hawked giraffes he'd carved from mukwa to tourists from South Africa. South African money put him through high school in the town at the end of the tar road. And when the manila envelope came from the university, his father went out and killed that lazy, lagging old ox. And then there was whistling teeth and the music of the *mbira* and ululating tongues and jouncing bones and sour beer.

Now Nina halts to buy a pineapple from an old woman who knifes off the spiky skin for them.

They ride on again, sucking at the yellow pulp and tuning into the wry, haunting twanging of Ry Cooder's guitar.

– It's a mystery. This isn't pineapple country. Only thing yellow you tend to find here is sunflowers, or the yellow sign of a Shell garage. Just the other day I heard a hadeda ibis calling in my yard in Cape Town. It's as if the compass in their head's fucked. There didn't used to be hadedas so far south.

She lifts the hem of her shirt to mop juice from her chin. Her low-slung jeans let out a rumour of hair.

His cock unfurls as he gazes out the window at the flat, stark land where opal-toned bones blink in the sun and lone birds ride the wires.

His forehead drums against the window as she swings the Pajero off the tar.

He winds down the window to gasp for air.

She kills Cooder.

For a moment the world's violently still. Then he hears the wind hum along the telegraph wires. And then he hears her husky breath in his ear.

She slides his pineapple-sticky hand under her panties. She's humid after the coolness of the pineapple.

He's perky as a meerkat now.

She unzips him and slides her lips over him. A bus blares its horn at them. The Pajero shudders in the gusty wake of the bus.

She licks her lips and pops another half-moon of pineapple into her mouth.

Then the Pajero's gunning south again.

He smells her on his fingers.

She's humming along to an Eels song.

He flicks through the sun-warped novel by Coetzee she has bird-winged on the dash. Yet Thokozile's eyes come between him and the out-of-focus words on the paper. He flicks to the cover and studies the image of a raw-boned fugitive dog on a dirt road. *I am that lost dog*, he thinks.

17

Hermanus. Noon.

    I stand before the house of the glass-eyed priest Zero said would hand his Vespa over to me. The sign on the gate tells me to BEWARE OF THE DOG. I can hear Chopin played poorly on the piano. I call *hello*. A butcherbird flies from the gutter.

No hiatus in the playing. And no sign of the dog. A rusty hand mower is islanded in long grass. An old black bicycle with a basket up front leans against the wall.

The gate whines like an old man's bones. I go along crazy paving through the high grass to the door. There's a pane of opaque glass in the door. I ring the doorbell. The piano fades out. A warped shadow ghosts towards me.

The priest in a frayed dog collar and long, colonial khaki shorts. I can't tell which eye is glass.

– I'm Jerusalem. I've come for the Vespa. My old man called you up from Cape Town.

– Aha. Cupido? The Vespa's in the garage.

– Where's your dog?

– Out in the backyard. He's old and stone deaf. He used to love Chopin. Now he can't tell Mozart from Masekela.

We go round to the back of the house. The priest has a faintly fascist way of throwing his feet out ahead of him.

On seeing a stranger, the dog jerks to his feet and barks a frenzied, gut-swinging, ball-jiggling volley. The priest puts out his hand to calm his old yellow lab.

– Don't mind him. It's just an act.

The dog follows us to the garage, snuffing at my heels.

A butcherbird is a peg on the clothes line.

A rat runs along the rim of the zinc backyard fence.

The dog goes after the rat and clangs his feet against the zinc. The butcherbird flies away.

– I hate that bird, says the priest. He dives and pecks at all the other birds.

In the garage there's an old MG and the Vespa. The Vespa is a perky red.

– She's beautiful, isn't she? I take her out for a run every now and then, but I'm losing feeling under my feet. It's a mystery . . . and they haven't found a cure. The doctor forbade me to ride.

He runs his fingers around the chrome rim of the headlight.

– I had hoped my son would want her, but he's not coming home.

– Where's he?

– London. He's a money man. Thinks this country has gone to the dogs.

Then, sensing how racist this sounds:

– Oh, I'm sorry. That's not how I see things. Yet I do fear for the future. So far the Xhosas have outwitted the Zulus. Mandela and Mbeki were wily. But I prophesy the Zulus won't bow to the Xhosas forever. Historically they are the warrior tribe. And now Zuma is jousting the Zulu spear at the sky.

– He's a clown.

– But he can dance a Zulu war dance and sing a song calling for his gun. And he has a grassroots following. And Africa has a habit of shooting herself in the foot. My son begs me to go to London. He'd put me up in his attic in Camden. I'd have no dog, no yard, no freedom to follow a road along the lagoon on a whim or walk along the beach for miles. London's no life for me. All the wan faces on the tube, sandwiched like grey ham between pages of the newspaper.

– I spent my young boyhood in Amsterdam. I remember the cold gnawing at my ears and toes. I remember the empty playgrounds in winter. I remember the steep stairs and how my socks never dried.

And I remember how folk never smiled in the winter. I remember a Moroccan whore in a pink-lit fish tank whom Zero paid to show me her buoyant tits. I was just eleven. He was worried I'd turn out gay.

– That's the other thing. Stairs. I have not told my son I have to focus just to walk along a flat path.

I hand over Zero's wad of rubber-banded rands to him. He pockets the money without thumbing through it.

– If you're ever lonely, come over for tea. I vow not to lure you into my church.

I hop onto the Vespa.

– She's been a good girl. You keep an eye on her. The roads are hazardous with all the jaywalking dogs and the crazy taxivans.

His eyes glisten as he bids his Vespa farewell. His dog, sensing his master's maudlin mood, licks his scabby shins.

18

Somewhere south of Bloemfontein.

The Pajero sharks on along the N1 through the Karoo. An arid land of lone windmills flashing steel petals to draw sheep to water tapped from dark, unseen rivers.

Now and then a deserted road dusts away from the highway.

The tarmac ahead is quicksilvery under the sun. That's perhaps why Nina doesn't see the karakul sheep in time to dodge it. Or perhaps it's the marijuana in her blood that blurs her senses. Either way, the Pajero's front fender flips the sheep high into the sky.

Jabulani and Nina tilt their heads in sync to follow the fight of the sheep till it vanishes overhead. Then they swivel their heads to see it land on the tarmac behind them.

Nina swings the Pajero hard off the tar. It spurts up dust. The motor stalls.

– Fuck, tunes Nina. I never saw it.

All you hear is the silver-winged tones of R.E.M. gliding out over bleak veld, over distant, earthed sheep.

They climb out and walk up to the sheep. It is still breathing, in jerky gasps. Its feet are folded up neatly under it. Its wool has no hint of blood in it. The only sign that it has just flown over a Pajero is a stoned look in eyes curiously free of accusation.

Nina tips up her shades to stare deep into its glassy eyeballs.

– We can't just ride on. It's got to be bleeding inside.

– You think so? It looks unscratched.

– It's in pain. I can tell from the eyes. We have to put it down.

– Kill it?

– A mercy killing.

– How do you intend to kill it?

– I've never killed a thing in my life. Other than ants and mosquitoes. You'll have to kill it.

– Me?

– *Ja.* You're from Zim.

– So?

– You had to fight for freedom. And now Mugabe's gone apeshit. You're used to violence.

– But I'm a teacher. I'm against violence.

Jabulani thinks: *Well, I have killed half-dead rats that the cat left bleeding in the yard. And I have twisted the head off a bird or two that few into the windscreen of my old Datsun. But this is killing on another scale. Just look at the size of its head.*

– This animal's in pain, man.

– Why me?

– I beg you to. Kill it for me.

Jabulani thinks: *If not for her I'd be dead.*

– Okay. I'll do it. For you.

Jabulani walks along the roadside till he finds a big stone. He lugs it over to the sheep. The stone has the heft of a medicine ball.

He stands over the sheep, focusing on his target: that flat hard plane between its eyes. He wonders how thick the skull is, and if it will crack in one go.

He thinks to himself: *Just half a year ago I stood in front of a class with a book in hand, teaching poetry. I taught my students how a line can see-saw on a comma and how words at the end of a line want to fall. I told them words have memory, music . . . and weight.*

The sheep's eyes glaze over now with a saintly pity for the lot of a teacher who must put poetry into the heads of schoolboys. It is a harder task, perhaps, than caving in a skull bone with a stone.

He lifts the stone.

Nina plugs her ears with her fingers and squinches her eyes shut.

After a time, she squints to see if the sheep's dead yet.

Jabulani's still holding the stone in his hands. And the sheep's not dead.

– I'm sorry. Its eyes spook me out.

– Don't be a pussy.

– Tell you what I'll do. I'll run it over. Then I don't have to look it in the eyes as it dies.

– That's genius.

– But you have to direct me. I want to hit its head just one time.

– Got it.

Jabulani gets in behind the wheel. He mutes R.E.M. Another volatile silence.

Overhead a vulture loops lazily.

The Pajero catches. He turns his head to get his bearings. Nina's a few yards beyond the sheep, hands poised in the air. He shifts the Pajero into reverse and its tyres kick up dust till they find tar. Now he's barrelling along. He focuses on Nina's waving hands rather than on the sheep. He flinches, gearing himself for the jolt of rubber against head, for a bang against the axle if his aim is marginally off.

Nina hops clear as he shoots by. She's yelling her head off.

He feels no jarring.

And yet the sheep's gone.

Jabulani thinks: *Perhaps the rear fender swept it up, like a cow-catcher. But I'd have felt it, wouldn't I? A sheep's not all wool.*

Then he sees it a few yards away, a bit bemused by the antics of men.

So it was just winded, after all.

Nina is keeling over, hooting with laughter.

Jabulani finds it less funny.

At a Shell garage a man in red overalls lures the Pajero to a diesel pump.

The name on his overalls is Othello. Jabulani wonders how a man in this random backwater came by such a name.

While Othello checks the oil and water, Jabulani goes to piss.

He is staring at a black target fly painted on the white china when he hears a shot. He swings on his heels and pees on his All Stars. He falls to the floor and peers out under the door.

Othello's down. A shot to the head. Nina runs towards the kiosk. Another shot spins and flips her like a rag doll.

Jabulani sucks a dry gasp down.

Ghost Cowboy hovers over her as he reloads. He lets the shot shells fall.

Then he stalks the kiosk, his gun levelled at the man behind the till. The man holds his hands up high.

Jabulani hops up on a toilet lid and climbs out the window. The window is the size of an A3 paper and he has to tilt his collarbones

TROY BLACKLAWS

towards the corners. Somehow he wiggles through, but his left All
Star catches on the window hook and peels off his foot. He wa-
vers, hoping to fish it out, until he hears another shot. He hops
and weaves over abandoned car skeletons and spirals of rusty wire.
Stones and glass and iron bolts jab at the sole of his left foot. At the
far end of the junkyard he vaults a zinc wall and slides down a slope
to the dry floor of a river. On this sand he can run freely.

The river sand flows to a pipe under the highway. He'd tunnel
into the dark if his footprints were not a dead giveaway. Instead, he
claws his way up to the tar road. He hears the rumble of a diesel
motor and instinctively ducks. Yet the thing barrelling towards him
is so absurd he has to laugh. He wonders if he's dreaming. He rubs
his eyes, then jives this madman war dance to catch the eye of the
psychedelic VW Kombi. A blurred canvas of painted flowers hums
by, then farts to a halt further along the road.

Jabulani turns to see Ghost Cowboy down in the riverbed coming after him. He's lost the shotgun and has a Colt revolver in hand.

Another shot. Pain stings through Jabulani's left hand.

Jabulani runs for the Kombi. He hears the Kombi catch and
chug yet a few yards further. His heart sinks. The bastard's changed
his mind. Then the Kombi door slides open for him. Then he's
running alongside the Kombi. He feels as if he's acting in a cowboy
flick. The guy's free hand is cajoling crazily. Yet another shot flicks
off the wing mirror. Jabulani dives in.

The guy hits the gas.

Jabulani juts his head out the door to see Ghost Cowboy standing on the tar road. Then he slides it shut.

– Fuck, tunes the guy behind the wheel. How'd you piss him off?

– He hunts Zimbos.

– You Zimbabwean?

– I am.

84

– Zim's smoked, brother.

Looking out on this bleak, sun-stung land, a dog-tired Jabulani thinks: *And South Africa's no merry-go-round so far.*

He holds his hand high to stay the blood. Still it slurs down his arm. He wonders: *Why this left jinx? Left All Star gone. Left hand shot.*

The guy tugs a bandana off his head.

– Name's Jake. Bind your hand with this till we get to a hospital.

– Freedom, says Jabulani.

– Hey?

– Name's Freedom. Jabulani Freedom Moyo.

– Freedom? Far out!

Jabulani winds the cloth around his hand and tugs it tight with his teeth.

– That's a hard-core motherfucker did that to you.

– I just saw him kill a man and a woman in cold blood.

– Where?

– At a Shell, just up the road.

– *Ai!* I was about to pull in to that garage. I'm running low on juice.

Jake taps the glass of the fuel gauge.

– But I thought I'd chance it to the next town. As I went by, a Land Rover painted like a zebra skin caught my eye.

– That's his.

Jake foots the pedal harder.

In their smoking wake a buzzard drops from the wires to yank at the rotting, flat carcass of an unlucky jackal.

19

Hermanus. Night.

After a short, hard rain I ride the Vespa on the Maanskyn-baai road out along the Hermanus lagoon. The moon lays down a fish-scale sheen on the slick tarmac. I dodge tyre grooves to avoid aquaplaning. I imagine Lotte riding pillion behind me, her hands on my hips.

At Vogelgat I shoot past a beer truck.

Over the Vespa's hum and the swish of her tyres I think I hear the piping, penny-whistle cry of a kingfisher. My eyes pan towards the lagoon.

Then there's a boy just ahead, eyes dazzled by my headlamp.

I veer away yet nick him with the running board, flipping him into a roadside gully.

The Vespa fishtails and I wipe out, careening over tarmac on a film of liquid. Tar peels my palm skin off.

The Vespa yells in a high, butcher-saw key. The headlamp flickers.

The beer truck hoots by.

I hobble to the gully but he's gone. No sign of him. I wonder if I dreamed him.

The Vespa cuts out. Tilting telegraph poles scratch the sky, screeching like chalk across a blackboard. I fall to my knees and retch into the dirt.

I fetch the Vespa and focus the headlamp on the gully. Then I see vermilion flecks of blood on the road. He'd gone over to the lagoon side. I walk the Vespa over to light up the wire fence. I see a hole in the wire and beyond it the headlamp draws a zigzagging white line. I wonder if buck or jackal wore this outlaw path flat.

I kill the light and abandon the Vespa.

I twist through the hole and follow the sandy, moonlit footway towards a scattering of beggarly gum trees. Their peeling bark bares pale flesh. The gums remind me of a colony of refugees in rags. Through the gums I catch glimpses of the moon dancing on the surface of the lagoon.

I walk in among the ghostly gums and rub my eyes at the surreal sight before me: a run-down, graffitied, double-decker London bus on fat, cracked tyres. Moonlight spiderwebs across stoned windows and tricks a cicada into going *chirr chirr* as if it is noon. A London bus in the *bundu*, a cicada serenading the moon. The world's gone haywire.

I step up onto the landing (half gearing myself for an Indian man to demand a pound for a ticket to Blackhorse Road). The bus is gutted and zoned off into boxes with cardboard and canvas. I am spooked by the myriad voodoo-vibe things hanging from the surviving roof rail: dolls short of a limb, spinning guineafowl-feather dreamcatchers, a phoenix cut out of a Fanta can, lone flip-flops, strings of *perlemoen* shells and bent driftwood, an enamel teapot, the jaw of a fish.

A boy sifts out of shadow as seamlessly as a chameleon shifting through shades of colour. Then there's another. Then another. And another. Till half a dozen boys in tatty shorts and dirty T-shirts gawp at me.

– Have you seen a boy who got hurt? I hit him on the road. He must be bleeding.

Their wide eyes are unblinking, wary. I sense they have all been hoodwinked and hurt by men.

– I am not from the police. I won't tell about the bus.

One of the boys, donning a black Kangol hat, signals with sliding eyes to a far corner of the bus.

The boy is curled up in a corner. His head is bleeding. His shorts are torn and clayey. His shins are skinned pink.

– I'm sorry. I took my eyes off the road.

He just stares at me.

– May I take you to a hospital?

– No doctor. I have no passport.

– Come to my flat then. I'll nurse you.

– Forget me, master. The pain will go.

– I am not your master. And I can't forget you. Where are you from?

– I am from Tanzania.

– How did you get here?

– I walked.

Back in my flat I pour hot water into the basin and tip a dose of Dettol in it. Then I wipe the sand out of the boy's pink-raw wounds with a cloth. Though he finches he does not cry. I dab Mercurochrome on his shins and bind a bandana around his head. His skull feels cool under my hand.

He stares at the weird pencil figures I drew on the wall but offers no verdict.

– What is your name?

– Buyu.

– I am Jerusalem.

– We sang a song called Jerusalem in the mission school in Tanzania. Is it a name for a man?

– For this one.

I laugh and then wince as the Mercurochrome stings my flayed palms and rubbed-up hip.

– How do you survive in Hermanus?

– I find golf balls in the water. Like a flamingo, I seek with my toes in the mud. If I am lucky I find maybe six or seven in one day. Some boys, they are scared of the water. Of snakes and leguaans hiding under water lilies. All I fear is crocodile and here there's no crocodile. The caddies, they give me one rand for a ball if it has no cut in it. They sell the balls to the fat white men for double. If I sell to the white men myself and the caddies catch me, they will beat me hard.

– Well, from tomorrow you no longer have to find golf balls for fat white men. I have a job for you. You can lend me a hand in the market where I sell wire animals. You'll earn a third of my takings. And we'll find you a pair of shorts and a T-shirt or two. For now this will do.

I hand Buyu a faded T-shirt with a lotus flower on it.

– So how come you left Tanzania?

Buyu casts wary eyes at me.

– It is one long story.

– Tell me. I beg you.

– Tomorrow?

– Tomorrow.

20

A hospital somewhere south of Bloemfontein.

Outside: A Karoo roadside *dorp*. One of the far-apart, dud towns that bead the N1.

Inside: White walls. A grey lino floor. A skew crucifix. A dog-eared Bible. A lone gecko. No flowers.

The pain hauls Jabulani out of a morphine haze.

His hand is wound in layers of white cloth. A red poppy stains through.

Out the window of the hospital Jabulani sees jacaranda flowers flicker. A jet stream zips across a blue sky. Swifts sew up the pain of the world with invisible gut.

A white policeman has a curt word with the young black policeman at the door. He shuffles into the room and shuts the door behind him. His faded grey-blue uniform is the sole colour accent in the room, other than Jabulani's blood. It's as if he just walked into a black-and-white film.

The name on his uniform: DE LA REY.

Jabulani has a hazy memory of learning that a De la Rey was a Boer hero of the war for freedom from the English.

– Doctor tells me a bullet took just a pig-ear chink out of your left hand. Cowboys and Indians, hey?

De la Rey mimics a boy's way of shooting: *bang bang.*

– Hardly chipped a bone. What are the chances of that?

The policeman's antics draw no smile from Jabulani.

– That V of skin between your thumb and finger is gone . . . just where you'd lick the salt off before taking a swig of tequila.

– I'll have a scar.

– Let me tell you, man. No one rides for free.

De la Rey lifts his shirt to reveal a messy scar in the drum-skin vellum of his beer gut.

– This was a bowie.

Perhaps feeling he's detoured from duty, De la Rey lets his shirt fall. He takes a notebook out of his pocket and a pencil from behind his ear.

– So, tell me. What kind of gun shot you?

– A revolver of some kind.

– And the guy?

– He has flowing white hair and albino white skin. They call him Ghost Cowboy.

– Where you from?

– Africa.

– Cocky, hey?

– I am from Zimbabwe.

What's your name?

– Jabulani Freedom Moyo.

He records Jabulani's name in a plodding, square hand.

– Profession?

– Teacher.

– A teacher, hey?

– English.

– Where's your passport?

– They took it.

– Who took it?

– Ghost Cowboy and the marijuana men.

De la Rey laughs.

– This is South Africa. Not Colombia.

– This Ghost Cowboy is no phantom. He shotgunned down a beautiful woman who picked me up in her Pajero.

– Beautiful?

– She was. He shot her at a Shell up the road. And he killed a petrol jockey called Othello.

– Othello?

– And now he's hunting me.

Again the policeman laughs.

– You sound as if you smoked some of that marijuana.

But this time he jots a few words in his notebook.

In a bid to justify Jonas's faith in him he tells his story, culminating in the Shell killings.

– You a Tarantino flick junkie?

– If you check it out you'll find her and the petrol jockey shot. And perhaps the man in the kiosk.

– Perhaps?

– I just heard the shot. I never saw him go down.

– I heard on the radio there was a shooting. I'll check it out. This Pajero chick. You learn anything about her?

About Nina-for-now? That she was a crazy live-wire girl. That she

92

loved Nina Simone. That she smoked grass. That she had me in her mouth and sent me floating.

– Just that she's from Cape Town. What will happen to me?

– Maybe they deport you. Maybe they jail you. Maybe they put you in the dock as a witness to this shooting. Maybe you lucky again and they hand you asylum papers . . . but that's a long shot.

Just then a blackbird pecks at its refection in the windowpane. The comical futility of this duel has the two men smiling at each other. Again the policeman feels he is letting himself drift into too matey a mode with this outlander. His smile fades out.

– So. Tell me. Why are you in this country?

– I lost my job. Times are hard under Mugabe.

– *Ja.* It's a pity. It was a paradise. I went fishing in Kariba one time. And I saw the Victoria Falls. Most amazing thing I ever saw. *The smoke that thunders,* you people call it, hey? But can you imagine how Livingstone felt? To be the man who discovered them.

– They'd been found before.

– Fact is, your country's fucked up now. And you can hardly blame Livingstone for that. Look, I feel for you, man . . . but you can't just waltz across the border.

He swings his hand in the air, as if to draw the borderline with his pencil.

– I was once in your shoes. I went to London when South Africa was still a bastard in the eyes of the world. I was on a tourist visa and forbidden to seek a job. I went from pub to pub . . . but they just shunted me on. I tell you, the line between me and the beggars in the Underground became thin as fishing gut.

The policeman pockets his notebook and pencil, abandons his bid to stay focused.

– I was staying with other South Africans, see, so I had a roof over my head and I never starved. But being put down again and again plays havoc with your ego, hey. In the end I boarded a plane home to South Africa. I never told folk this end that I didn't find a job overseas. I never told them London beat me down till I cracked. I tell my wife and my sons it was the cold and the quirky ways of the English. So I will stay in this town till I die. Here I'm a hero. I draw my gun on whoever holds up the 7-Eleven. I shoot them dead if I have to. Like I did that bastard who stabbed me.

– I am scared of the things ahead.

– But you have something going for you I never had.

– I do?

– *Ja*. You've read books. You have studied.

– You never read?

– Not deep books. Just crime. I'm reading a hard-core crime novel now. You find yourself rooting for the killer in a land where justice is a joke. He goes after the kind of men who think fucking a virgin will cure you of The Virus. He's my hero, that bloke.

– You are not a stereotypical policeman.

De la Rey laughs.

– I got one of my men posted by your door. His job is to prevent you from running away while I verify your story. And to fend off *ghost cowboys*.

Again he forms an imaginary gun and goes *bang bang*.

– If I find this Shell story happened the way you tell it, I'll look into this marijuana farm shit. Either way I may have to handcuff you. You catch my drift?

He walks up to the window.

– I reckon a man'd survive falling out this window. With a bit of luck.

It's not hard for Jabulani to get the hint.

21

Hermanus.

Buyu's story:

– My father, he was a fisherman.

– Lake Victoria?

– Yes. Him and his father before him.

– My forefathers were fishermen too. They fished for *snoek* in the Atlantic.

Buyu smiles at this twinning of our roots.

– My father, he fished for tilapia from his dhow. One day the white man, he came along and tipped a bucket of river fish into the lake and the river fish killed all the lake fish.

– *River* fish?

– They call him Nile perch.

– I heard perch can become as long as a man.

– Longer still. So now my father, he caught too few fish for my mother to sell in the market. Outsiders came to catch the giant river fish from trawlers. If a tilapia fisherman wanted to catch a river fish, the trawler men shot at him. My father's dhow stayed on the beach. For money for my school uniform and schoolbooks he dived into the lake to herd the river fish into the nets of the trawlers. For this the trawler men handed him a few pennies. With this money you could not buy a bottle of milk or a bag of *sadza*, never mind books. Still, he hoped to survive this way . . . until a crocodile took his foot off.

– No way!

So Zero was lucky just to have lost half his calf to a shark.

– Now we had no money. My mother, she went to the fish factories that gut the river fish to send overseas. She begged for a job but they said there was no job for her. Like a begging dog she went barefoot over pyramids of stinking throwaway fish to pick the bones.

He draws in air and blinks his eyes rapidly.

– Then one day the factory men, they came to our hut in a pickup. They dragged my mother howling out. They shot guns at the sky. My father, he hopped after them on his good foot, shaking his stick at them. One of the factory men then shot at the sand by his feet and my father, he did this jerky dance. The factory men, they laughed like hyenas.

– That's fucked up.

– When they had gone my father, he fell over and rubbed sand on his head.

– Was there nothing your father could do?

– He went to the police. They told him they would put him in jail if he made mischief. He went to the factory and the guards beat him with sticks. After that he just sat on the sand by his dhow and looked out over the lake. If the sky above was pink with flamingos, if a neighbour put a bowl of sour beer down for him, if young girls skipped over a rope tied to the mast of his dhow, he would just go on looking ahead of him. In the end my hope for him was torn as the sail of his dhow.

I picture a worn-out sail flapping on a loose boom.

– And your mother?

– After half a year the factory men, they offloaded her. Her hair was gone and her dress hung loose. My father, he would not let her into his hut. He said he was no longer a man and so he had no wife. She camped in the dhow on the sand. I lay with her. She begged me to go south. In South Africa, she said, there is gold under the sand. And diamonds. And when the wind blows, oranges and avocados fall and rot in the sun. In South Africa the seas are full of fish. They chuck the fish heads along with the guts to the birds. In South Africa the white men throw out the feet of a chicken. In South Africa men may not shoot their guns at the sky and snatch girls who catch their eye. The law forbids it. And if you have this thing I have, she said, they give you medicine so you can survive to see your son finish school. So I told her I will go to this land of gold and oranges and find medicine for her.

– How'd you survive the long trek?

– I hid in holes, cracks and empty shacks. I ate insects, worms and rats. Whatever I could catch. In Zambia one time a stray dog followed me for two days. In the end I picked up a stone and put it in my bag. I climbed a tree and waited. In the end that dog, he got too curious and came to sniff the air and looked up at me. I let the stone go. He fell over. I came down and hit him on the head with that stone until his feet no longer kicked. I was hungry and wanted to cut him up, but I was scared of the evil in him. And in Zimbabwe on the border crazy guys called *gumagumas* hunted me. I hid in an empty warthog hole and prayed to Jesus, for he too came out of the hole they put him in.

22

A hospital somewhere south of Bloemfontein.
The nurse had put a tray down, across Jabulani's lap. Under the teacup he finds a wisp of paper torn from the margin of a newspaper.

Hey Dude. I begged a nurse to hand this to you. I'm @ motel as you head out of town. Room 9. Kombi's out back. If you want a ride, catch me by sundown. Jake

Jabulani hops out of bed and lets his hospital frock fall. He tugs on his jeans and shirt. He snatches frog-green rubber hospital clogs.

From the window he lets the clogs fall two floors. They skip off the hard tarmac of the parking lot, then land toe to toe. Jabulani interprets this as a good omen. He slides out over the sill. He holds onto the window frame with his good hand till he hears a shot from somewhere in the hospital. He falls.

Pain knifes up through his shins and he flips over on the tar like that *pangaed* woman tossed from a pickup by Mugabe's monkeys. Blood filters through the white cloth on his hand.

He hears another shot. The black policeman at the door will have gone down.

He picks up the clogs and darts barefoot across the lot. At the far end he hides behind a parked taxivan, gulping air and feeling the clogs on to his feet while he scans the hospital through the tinted glass of the taxivan. Amazingly a taximan is dozing at the wheel while Lucky Dube howls from the radio. Jabulani sees Ghost Cowboy at the window of his hospital room, panning his hawk eyes across the lot.

Then the barrel of a gun is at Ghost Cowboy's eye and a bullet skips off the roof of the van.

The taximan shoots out of the van like a fat seed popped from a pod and, lying as flat as his beer gut will let him, calls out to God: *Tixo! Tixo!*

The sight is so comical Jabulani laughs a knee-jerk laugh.

The next shot scatters glass.

A siren joins Lucky Dube in a jarring duet. Ghost Cowboy vanishes from the window.

Jabulani dances over glass diamonds in his hospital clogs. A shard of glass spikes through the rubber into his sole-skin. Pain flares through his jinxed left foot. He gimps along on the other foot as he plucks out the glass.

Then he's out of the lot and hop-jogging down the road, past a hotel where a dun man studies a fly drowning in his beer, sidestepping an old grandpa who is spitting blood into his hanky, hurdling the cardboard box of a pink-turbanned fruit seller who sells avocados, dodging a dog that clacks his teeth at his heels and an old woman who jousts her walking stick at him and yells: *Bliksem! Hoodlum! Catch him!*

Now he's running full speed on a volatile high of pain and fear. He topples a cart, sending oranges rolling across the tarmac. He outruns a black priest in black garb on a bicycle who calmly doffs his hat to him as if this is a common sight: a man hurtling by at full tilt, casting haunted eyes behind him.

At the motel he raps on the door to room No. 9. A maid eyes him skewly.

He gasps wordlessly.

She snatches up her mop in case he goes for her.

Jake swings the door open. There's a fake tiger skin on the wall and a porn video on the TV. A girl's riding a white horse bareback on the beach. She has zilch on. Just tits bobbing to a *Bonanza* kind of rhythm and red hair flowing like a river.

Jake hands Jabulani a half-jack of cheap whisky.

Jabulani shakes a dose of whisky over his bleeding foot. It stings like blazes. Then he swigs a shot to dull the throbbing in his hand and slow the spinning of his head.

– That Cowboy's after me again.

– Let's go, Freedom, my man.

They don't even wave goodbye to the naked rider.

Outside the door the maid swings her mop up again. They go through a gap to the back where the VW hobnobs with a rusting, bleeding Dodge up on bricks. A cat jumps out of the Dodge, spooking Jabulani and Jake.

– You take the Dodge, Jake jokes.

Jabulani is gobsmacked by Jake's cool. But then he did not see that Zimbabwean shotgunned down in cold blood. Nor Nina rag-dolling.

23

Hermanus market.
Buyu's all natty in his plaid Oakley shorts and Quiksilver T-shirt.

I teach him how to hang up the seahorses and whales and how to lay out the animals (geckos in front and giraffes behind). I put them in rows: birds of a feather.

He jumbles them up, subverting all sense of scale.

I teach him how much each goes for and how much leeway he has for haggling.

He tells me if I just sit and hope folk will walk up to the stall, I will die a poor man. He heads off with a penguin in one hand and a gecko in the other.

There's a pungent tang of sea in the wind. Pink-footed pigeons bob and coo on the zinc roof of the Fisherman's Cottage.

And the same unflinching sun fades the tarps and umbrellas cast over the stalls and peels the paint off bone-toned walls. And the same fruit seller calls his unvarying shrill litany.

The dreadlock dude sways listlessly as a jaded go-go girl as he juggles his devil sticks.

And Hunter whistles tunelessly as she shines her tiger's eyes, moonstones, ambers and fossils with the same dazed look in her eyes.

Beyond her the man from Senegal barters with a tourist who hovers over him as he paints his cast of two-foot-high characters.

I love this raw, haphazard poetry of the market. Each stall a stanza: measured out and lone-standing yet somehow overlapping and running on. I wonder how I spent years in the muted, stale time-warp of a library while all along life . . .

A whistled chirp from Hunter cuts this thought short. I focus to see the glass-eyed priest slope up to my stall.

I am scared he'll wonder how I got scratched up and so discover I dinged his Vespa.

But he just dandles a gecko unhandily, as if in a daze.

– My dog's gone. Something's happened to him.

Hunter abandons her stone-rubbing to tune in.

– He wanders down the road, but he's never strayed for long. If he'd got run over, I'd have found him. It's a mystery.

– Maybe he smelt a bitch and lost his head, chirps Hunter.

The priest coughs a curt laugh.

– He's seventy-seven in dog years. For him and his master, the days of courting girls are long gone.

Hunter sighs. She shuffles over, holding out a quartz to him.

– Ever seen a wisp of smoke forever captured in hard water?

He peers into the quartz as if looking for evidence of God.

– You may think I'm mad . . . but I think they thought he was a stray. And I think someone's hunting the street dogs in this town.

I want to laugh, but I see he's not joking.

– They all used to beg for fish guts at the new harbour . . . but now you hardly ever see them.

I realise that I've not seen the pariah market dogs since the afternoon Zero dropped me off.

– They took him. That's my theory.

In a bid to be breezy, I joke:

– Why would they? This isn't Vietnam. Or China.

But Hunter *sabos* my shot at breeziness:

– Maybe they inject them with heroin in the townships to see how pure it is before shooting up.

The priest sways as if he's on the verge of keeling over.

– Or that Chinaman Foo Buck Koon turns them into soy-doused take-away?

I glare at her for being too glib. Yet the priest hardly hears her.

– I heard there's a demand for killer dogs in Johannesburg, he says in a wavering voice. He's got guts. I've seen him kill a porcupine.

I dare not tell him his deaf, spent dog would be hopeless as a guard dog.

– Maybe witch doctors want him for their voodoo *muti*, Hunter pipes up again.

God fops out of the priest's mouth like a spat-out fish.

Hunter's in a groove:

– They turn their bones into a kind of snuff. Or scientists caught him. They don't just shoot dogs into space, they use them as guinea pigs to find a cure for malaria and yellow fever.

Again the priest says *God*.

Instead of soothing him Hunter reels off her cryptic mantra:

– Things can get hazardous.

I turn to the priest.

– Hey, I'll keep an eye out for him.

At that moment the harbour hobo heads for his fig tree, cup in hand. He slides his spine down the bark. Moonfleet folds at his feet.

The priest gazes glumly at the dog.

– Dogs all over this country. Why'd they snatch mine?

Tears bead down his cheek till his stubble pops them. He rubs his eyes with the heel of his hand.

– Let me make you a sweet cup of tea, coos Hunter.

She taps hot water from a flask into a cup and drops a used tea bag into it.

– He loved haring after seagulls on the beach. He'd skip through the waves after a tennis ball. He was plucky. Now I have no one to play my piano for.

An old, one-eyed priest playing the piano for a deaf dog. A woman murmuring to dumb garden gnomes. Another lamenting a lost beauty to dead stones. A *muezzin*'s cry falling on deaf ears. Rocking men reeling off prayers to a god who turned a blind eye last time.

Hunter teaspoons Peel's honey into his tea, stirs it, then hands it to him. As he slips a finger through the ear of the teacup, she runs her fingers along his hand.

Just then Buyu jogs up, waving a fistful of notes at me.

– You see!

– I see.

– I got *double* what you wanted for the things. *Double!*

– But that's unethical.

Buyu laughs his white-white teeth at me.

– They went smiling away.

I tell the priest this is Buyu, who walked all the way from Tanzania.

– I see you two have been in the wars.

As a red herring I sing out:

– Buyu and I will find out what happened to your dog. Hey, Buyu?

Buyu flicks me a mock salute.

– That's kind of you. Goodbye, Jerusalem. Goodbye, Buyu. And thank you for the tea, ma'am.

– Call me Lily, Hunter says.

– Lily. A beautiful name, he says as he goes.

Lily zero-mindedly shines the teacup with her rubbing cloth.

– How do we find a dog, Buyu?

He frowns as if figuring out a hard sum. Then his eyes spark.

– We go to the boys!

– Hey?

– The bus boys! They know every alleyway, every kitchen courtyard, every dustbin with no lid on. They have learnt to think like dogs.

– Cool.

– We'll get them Kentucky, hey?

Just then the whale crier's kelp horn sounds.

– The world's gone haywire, says Hunter. The whales used to head south again for the Antarctic by the end of September. Then a few calving mothers stayed over Christmas. And now the dogs are vanishing.

– You think there's a plot?

– Something's awry. It may not be human.

– You mean black magic?

– I told you, things can get hazardous. Anything can happen.

I wonder if my mother can stop falling further out of focus. I wonder if Buyu and I can find the priest's dog. Most of all, I wonder if Lotte can happen and how on earth I am to woo her shadowed by a ragtag boy and fairy-godmothered by a seller of fossils.

Shadows of seagulls drift and dart over the market floor.

A breeze sweeps along dust and longing.

24

Cape town. Dusk.

The fabled flat-spined mountain is a giant stone dragon rimmed with an orange haze.

Jake's Kombi heads past the harbour of cranes and ship funnels and yacht masts jousting haphazardly. Sea tang, dockyard din and gull yells gust in through the wound-down windows. And out flow the jiving tones of Bafo Bafo at full volume.

Sails drift to and fro on the sea. Jabulani's eyes are agape at the wonder of this duned, inverted sky.

And that flipped copper coin gone all verdigris is Robben Island, where they jailed Mandela for so long.

They hum along Strand Street, under tall palms dancing in the wind. Barefoot street boys laugh and whistle at the crazy-coloured Kombi singing by.

At robots they are hustled by boys jockeying to hawk things crafted from wire and men yelling the headlines or wanting to wipe dust-filmed windows.

Jabulani sees a white man begging amid diesel fumes and dud dreams.

Now zero on this earth can amaze Jabulani.

He feels lucky to ride high – however fleetingly – in a world where folk are begging, burning out, being shot at.

In Sea Point Jake finds a free bay on the seafront. They pick up fish and chips from a van and a few beers from a bottle store. They dodge skaters and joggers on the seafront path and hop over the railings and perch on rocks rimed with salt and seagull guano. Jabulani slides his good foot out of a rubber hospital clog and into the cool of a rock pool. Seagulls bicker and beg for chips. Jabulani's beer can tips and beer froths out over the rocks like sea foam. He thinks of the blood spilt so he has the freedom to sit cooling his feet and filling his gut: *Poor Othello. Poor Nina. That man in the kiosk? The policeman in the hospital?*

Jabulani reads the news his fish and chips is wrapped in:

Nigerian pub ransacked

'Who are you? Where are you from?' This has become the war cry of the young men roving the townships, armed to the teeth with hoes, stones and guns. Their mission is to root out foreigners, to loot their shacks, to rape their women. The targeted come from Zimbabwe, Malawi, Mozambique, Tanzania, Kenya, Congo and beyond. Such foreigners, often in the country without a visa, are accused of taking locals' jobs. It seems that apartheid is far from dead. It has resurfaced as xenophobia: the fear of foreigners. Police are slow to deal with attacks such as this one on an unlicensed Nigerian-run pub in Langa.

A police captain said: 'Illegal foreigners have a penchant for crime. They don't pay tax and they try to be clever by producing fake papers.'

The Nigerian pub keeper, who was formerly a journalist in Lagos, said: 'I came to South Africa to escape persecution. I never thought this would happen in the country of Mandela.'

In downtown Cape Town, Bishop Tutu called for calm.

The sea flings white foam at the sky and the foam sticks like wet paper to form clouds.

Jabulani thinks of how this cockroachy thing called racism will always survive, somehow, in one form or another. He fears this rancour towards African foreigners they call *makwerekwere . . .* towards him: job-pincher, tax-dodger, would-be thief and paper-faker. The fear of this racist venom is as biting as the bullet wound in his hand. He shakes his head and focuses on the waves.

Their mad, macho fervour followed by a sighing, ebbing lull echoes the universal rhythm of wanting and sating. For now his hunger is stilled, but he wants an end to the throb of pain in his hand. And he has other wants. He wants to love his wife under a free sky. He wants to go on holiday to the seaside with Panganai and Tendai, for them to see this vista of shifting blue dunes and a diving sun. He wants to teach again, in a world where headmasters are not puppets of evil men and where boys and girls have the freedom to question the things they are taught. And where will a man find such a world if outsiders are hunted and shops burnt in this paradise called Cape Town?

Perhaps there's a place overseas somewhere where a man may live out his life fearlessly. But perhaps there, where they have no fear of guns and stones and evil men, they learn to fear other things.

— Beautiful, hey? chirps Jake.

— Beautiful. I wish they could see this.

— Your wife and kids? One day they will.

Jabulani shakes his head and laughs a hissing laugh.

— Hey. It may be a pipe dream now, but you were born under a lucky star. I feel it in my bones.

How, Jabulani wonders, will this pipe dream convert to reality? Another man has put fish and chips in his hands. He wears this man's shirt and jeans. He has no good shoes and not a cent to his name.

He flicks chips to the fussing, flapping seagulls. They swoop and catch midair.

To him the seagulls look like white crows. He imagines Panganai plucking his guitar and the seagulls diving to catch fragments of Marley.

And Jabulani dreams: There'll be sunshine and wine and jokes and he'll put his hands over Tendai's eyes and she'll peek through his fingers.

— Hey, Jabulani. A mate has a gig tonight. I said I'd go. You can come along and I'll foot the bill for a few beers. And maybe I can find you a room with one of my mates. You see, my flat's just a box. And my girlfriend's writing her thesis and . . .

Jabulani bends his head.

— She's funny that way. She needs her karmic space.

Jabulani sees how naive it was of him to imagine this guy would wave a magic wand and conjure a roof and a job for him.

— It's not that you're black. She'd just get weirded out by my pitching up with a refugee. I'm sorry.

— Hey, you have ferried me to Cape Town for no money. You have risked your life for me. You have revived my hope. I will never forget you.

CRUEL CRAZY BEAUTIFUL WORLD

– I'll just call in at the flat and then pick you up again. Stay where you are. *Ja*? I won't be long. And I'll lend you shoes. You look like a palooka in those things.

Now he's back-pedalling to the van.

– You just stay put. *Ja*?

When Jake pitches up with a gift of rugby jersey and white Havaianas flip-flops, Jabulani has vanished.

Jake parks off on the rocks, rolls a jay, and hangs his head and smokes that jay dead.

The frangipani-sweet fragrance of the marijuana drifts to where Jabulani hides.

Then Jake flicks the jay stub away and gets down from the rocks. He hangs the jersey over the railing, puts the flip-flops down. Then he yells:

– Good luck, Freedom!

Then he's gone.

Jabulani unwinds the bandage from his hand. He strips down to his jeans and wades into the sea. The jaggy pink bullet wound in his hand stings like blazes. It feels as if he's rubbing a chilli into it. Yet he holds his hand under, so the salt can heal. It stings so sore he hardly notices the footnote sting of the cut in his foot. Then the cold numbs the pain and he yields to the giddy high of having made it to Cape Town.

Now he's a boy in the sea, laughing as the waves flip over him.

He stays on the bench in the waning light till the wind blows his skin dry. Then he tugs on the rugby jersey. The dry salt on his skin catches slightly on the fabric. It smells of jasmine.

So subtly had their life become pared down to the bone over that last half-year in Zim. No flowery-smelling liquid to follow the Omo into the spinning drum, no sugar to sweeten the cheap coffee, no Johnnie Walker to dull the white noise of worry in his head.

He tears his old shirt and binds a strip of the cloth around his hand. He ties off the cloth with his teeth. He hoop-shoots a rubber clog at a wire bin on a lamp post. He scores. Then the other. This one dances on the rim before falling in. He interprets this as another good omen and smiles.

25

Hermanus new harbour. After dusk.

Buyu and I and the bus boys dangle feet from the harbour wall among hand-liners and languid lovers. They swig ice-cold Coca-Cola from cans and gnaw Kentucky off the bone. They throw bones to begging dogs and chips to cussing gulls.

From the gunwales of moored fishing boats cormorants forlornly eye us like some sorry Greek chorus. They spurn a flutter of fish tails under the hulls of the fishing boats.

The chief of the barefoot outcasts, in his dirty Kangol hat and boy-soldier shades, vows he'll keep his eyes peeled for dog hunters.

Buyu hangs out with the bus boys on the harbour wall while I play old standards on my guitar for tourists and old fogeys in a shacky joint called Quayside Cabin. I wonder if Zero would view old standards (*Hotel California, Bad Moon Rising, Sweet Home Alabama*) as trading goods.

The kitchen's in an old shipping container. From the roof hang fishing floats and other flotsam and funky junk. The girl waiters wear orange shirts. They are as boyish as hockey girls.

I play for free calamari and chips and tips. I play till my fingertips sting.

At midnight I find Buyu alone on the hull of a capsized trawler in dry dock. We share the calamari and chips. I think of my one-man play. It was staged in a dry dock at the Cape Town waterfront. It was interspersed with the barks of seals and the jeers of gulls.

A seal on the slipway honks at us and we flick him a bit of calamari. He just sniffs at it in a smirky way. He wants his fish raw. He slides sullenly into the harbour.

We lie down on the hull. Scorpio forms a stippled question mark on the blackboard of the sky.

– Buyu, I'm in love with a green-eyed girl.

– Where's she?

– Here in Hermanus.

– How come you hide her from me?

– She has a boyfriend.

– Shit.

– Yeah. Shit. I'm hooked, man. I'm bleeding, I tell you.

– No other girl is good?

– It's not *girl*. It's her.

– Then you have to catch her.

– How? I play my guitar and you dance like a monkey?

– I'm not your monkey.

– Sorry. It was a joke.

– Tell me her name.

I waver, scared the magic in her name will fade if I say it to another.

– Lotte.

– *Lo-ta.* Good for a song, hey?

I sigh.

– You go play again before they fire you.

When I come out again, I have a bottle of beer for me and a Fanta for Buyu and money in my pocket. It feels good to have earned the money, for the market takings are, at the end of the day, another of my old man's handouts.

A hunter's moon hangs over the harbour.

I sing and strum *Moonshadow* for Buyu. The sting in my fingertips is the sting of longing for Lotte.

A young whale blows in the harbour.

Buyu is up on his feet, dancing on the arced hull.

– Play, play, he cries. That whale, she loves your guitar.

Now I too am dancing on the hull under the moon, singing to a whale, wishing I had a way to tune into his undersea poetry.

The few folk still lingering over an espresso or a Don Pedro come helter-skeltering out of Quayside Cabin. They flash cameras and howl a hullabaloo till the whale dives and is gone.

Buyu and I ride the Vespa along the potholed roads of Zwelihle township. Hardly human figures slide along sandy paths through a maze of wonky tin-roofed shacks or hold hands out to the star-sparks of a brazier. Skinny dogs stalk the flickering firelight and bark at us out of the dark, but none look at all akin to a yellow, fat-gut lab. A whore slants against the door frame of a shack, advertising firelit skin. Two swaying men sing an off-key karaoke to a song on a radio: a yearning and sorrow no hooker can cure.

The fire and the dark, the moon and the sea, they tango on and on.

On the other side of the road sits one lone, tilting bivouac in a wasteland lot of cracked glass and wire snakes and half bricks. Maybe the hideout of a *sangoma*, a medicine man.

Or of a man whittled down to the bone by The Virus. Another snubbed, sidelined soul. It was always thus. It has yet to happen.

26

Long street, Cape Town.

Jabulani figures all the foreigners have a gig on the go. Glib-tongued traders sell marijuana, second-hand iPods, fake Ray-Bans and bootleg films from India. One capering fellow lures motorcars into parking bays with theatrical hand signals. Another wipes windows of motorcars free of sea salt and butterfly flecks. Another has revived the dead art of the shoeblack. Yet another dude in dirty dreads sounds his didgeridoo on a street corner, a haunting drone pervaded randomly by gull shouts and hooting and the clang of a church bell.

The world smells of sea and coffee and clammy skin and fallen flowers. And, absurdly, of hope. However dirt poor you are, however long since Lady Luck smiled on you, something in this town tells you that your fortunes may change at the drop of a hat.

He goes from bar to bar, coffee shop to coffee shop, bookshop to bookshop, in a bid to find a job. Again and again he is spurned. He can tell some folk find it forward of him to seek a job handling books and paper, china and teaspoons as a skint black man. They frown at his duds. Smirk at his flip-flops. They are wary of the litany of highbrow words at his fingertips. And warier still of his crook hand.

At the Long Street Bar he begs for a glass of water. A surly barman taps water into the glass and tells him to drink it outside, out on the pavement. Eyes at the bar glare low and leery over cold beer. He goes out and casts his eyes to the mountain. From this angle it is a vast iron anvil and it bears down on him, squeezing air from his lungs. He draws in a draft of dry berg wind chased by a swig of lukewarm water. No ice for him. He wants to fling the glass down on the paving to see shards scatter and blink in the sun. Instead he skulks through the bar gloom again and bows as he hands the man the glass. The eyes of the beer swiggers sweep him out.

He unwinds the cloth from his shot hand to air the wound.

A posse of Nigerians in tweed caps hangs out outside a bottle store. Their hands are never still. They shuffle wads of money, they flip and catch coins, they twiddle Rizla paper between thumbs and trigger fingers, they thumb lighter wheels to spit fire, they text one-handedly, their thumbs game-boying over the keys. When they catch him staring, one of them tells him to *piss off* and spits at him.

Jabulani is gobsmacked by this spat venom.

The spitter draws a knife and runs the back of the blade along his throat.

Jabulani spins on his heels and hotfoots it down Long Street in the goofy, jerky tempo of a silent movie.

The Nigerians fling jeers after him that may not crack his bones yet sting like peach stones.

He weaves through the canvas-roofed stalls of Greenmarket Square, where they sell masks and drums and cloths and carved animals and other bazaar curios. They are from Gambia, Senegal, Kenya, Tanzania . . . Timbuktu. White tourists who can't tell one black from another are fooled into imagining it is all South African art. A bone peddler sells fly-specked bones piled on newspaper. A travelling barber plies his trade under a beach umbrella. A Chinese *faf* man sells luck from a box.

– Dream of the moon, you bet on 9. Dream of a dog, you bet on 27. Dream of pussy . . . well then, you had your good time.

And it is then that he catches sight of a man whiter than any other. Ghost Cowboy standing in front of a stall that sells absurdly lanky giraffes carved out of wood in the Zimbabwean style.

Jabulani's blood runs cold.

Ghost Cowboy screws his right thumb into the palm of his left hand to describe Jabulani's stigmata hole to the stall keeper. Then he hands the man money and a scrap of paper. The man nods.

Jabulani slides his hands into his pockets and falls into a dead run along Shortmarket Street and then down Loop Street, where illegal aliens loll about, begging for jobs and smoking to kill time. He runs all the way down to the harbour, where seals slide into the sea as seagulls carp and tourists gawp and fishing boats bob shadowlessly under a zenith sun.

27

Hermanus market.

The scent of Hunter's *rooibos* tea reminds me of my mother reading to me in Amsterdam (*Of Mice and Men*, *The Old Man and the Sea*) and how she never folded down the corners but marked how far she'd read with a guineafowl feather instead. And how I begged her to tell me of South Africa and she'd tell me that if you filtered it all down you ended up with a blue sea and flower sellers in Adderley Street and *snoek* fishermen in Hout Bay and Zulu rickshaw men in Durban . . . and a hole dug by diamond hunters. All things spinning around a deep, deep plughole.

And always, *rooibos* tea and frangipani and the giddy smell of the sea.

And though the words and images eluded her, the murmuring cadences of my mother's voice sent my sister drifting into tulip-vivid dreams.

I am joggled out of reverie by her heading this way, by the swishing whisper of flouncy fabric against her skin, and by the telltale outline of a tanga.

Buyu follows her like a dog. For a moment I fear he'll sniff at her ass. I wonder how he senses this is her, my seagull girl.

– Hey. I heard you play your guitar the other day, in front of the Burgundy. And I was wondering . . .

A fermata: an unbearably sustained note.

– . . . if you'd play for me this Friday.

My heart goes haywire like a rat in a box.

Buyu nods frenziedly and hops from foot to foot behind her tangaed ass.

Words find it tricky to travel through my dry gullet:

– For . . . you? Just for you . . . alone?

She laughs that killing, pearly laugh again.

– I'm having a party. A few folk are coming out from Cape Town.

My heart flick-flacks. She's inviting me to her party!

– I thought it'd be cool to have live music.

Fool. She's not inviting me to hang out with her. She just wants me to amuse her friends. This casts me in another undefined limbo: I'll be neither guest nor servant. In a word, the problem of being *coloured* in South Africa under apartheid.

– How much do you charge?

Buyu's flicking his fingers to signal *mucho mucho* money.

– I play at Quayside for tips.

– He charges five hundred a throw. He's good, Hunter pipes up.

– Five hundred?

I glare at Hunter.

– We can haggle . . . if you want, I tell Lotte.

Zero's Survival Tip #2. *Moffied down.*

– He'd sell his mother for a pittance, Hunter flippantly footnotes.

Lotte squints her eyes. Amused? Bemused? Hard to tell.

– What kind of music do you play?

– All kinds, punts Buyu.

– I play folk rock. Indie, I'd say. I love The Black Keys. And I can do reggae.

– Can you play any Wilco?

– Just Kamera, from *Yankee Hotel Foxtrot*.

– Hey. You're tuned in.

– Tuned into what? Hunter quips in her wisecrack way.

– To find my place you just follow the path from the harbour towards Kwaaiwater. Come along after the market shuts down. You'll see fairy lights hanging in the yard. And a flowering frangipani.

I act witless to hide the fact that I have voyeured into her frangipani yard from the cover of milkwoods.

– Cool.

– Hey, I don't know your name.

– Jerusalem.

She arcs a brow.

– *Jerusalem?*

– You may call me Jero, if you'd rather. My old man does.

– No. Jerusalem's magic. There's music in it.

I feel as if a blade fan is spinning in my head. Or a seabird flapping his wings. *Whhhoooff. Whhhoooff. Whhhoooff.*

28

L ong street, Cape Town. Another day.

Jabulani breathes in a fusion of sea tang, coffee fumes and pigeon funk. He dodges the sassy boys who flick blades and barbs at him. He keeps his hands in his pockets and his eyes peeled for Ghost Cowboy.

He drifts among the skirted and spurned, the spat-on and burned, among the soot-handed and dust kissed: the flotsam of Africa forever waiting for Godot among pigeon feathers and fag stubs and dream shards, forever condemned to a gutter limbo. A hapless aura hangs off them like a tatty shadow.

Followed by their dazed eyes, he fears he'll end up as just such a gutter zombie, for he lacks a cocky faith in his fate. If Thokozile had not spurred him on, he'd never have embarked on this jinxed journey.

On another frequency he overhears fragments of frivolous café dialogue about films and music, about *The Beach* and Coldplay, about Tarantino and Oasis. To them, the mojito sippers and sushi junkies, the cursed and huddled are invisible. They tune out the jabberings of the beggars and prophets. They are as cool and aloof in their cooled cafés and capsuled bars as the white window dummies flaunting fine dresses his wife has never had money for.

He sees a stray dog pissing against a bicycle festooned with bags full of flotsam and junk.

He idly stares at a stub-footed man in aviator goggles jabbing a fist at the raging sun.

Echoes of his Zimbabwe waylay him. A woman with hair cornrowed like Thokozile's holding a newspaper as a parasol. A *penga* beggar crooning Bob Marley into the mouth of a beer bottle like a love-mad pigeon. A song by Zimbabwean singer Tuku on the radio. Warped figures sculpted from Zimbabwean stone lurking in a cool café courtyard. Jigsaw words in Ndebele painted on alley walls. The crazy laugh of a hoopoe, the bird they call *hleka mfazi* in his lingo. A young Zimbabwean called Zola catching a shaft of sun after a weekend in jail for loitering. Somehow between van and jail he had lost a shoe.

Jabulani and Zola and maybe a million other Zimbabwean interlopers all hustling for a foot in the door, for a handful of sand to put a shack on, for the freedom not to have to glance over your shoulder all the time.

At noon a cannon sounds on Signal Hill and folk down tools. Bricklayers and street sweepers lie flat on the pavement of Loop Street to doze.

Jabulani fishes a newspaper out of the bin to rest his head on. Then he too lies down flat on Loop and gazes up at the mountain. Up on slopes, beyond Jabulani's range of sight, stoned *bergies* hide from the burning sun under foraged skins of tarp. Jabulani's eyelids fall. Red sunlight flares through his thin lid-skin, so he turns his head to the side. He's about to glide into dream when a furry tail tickles his face. He smiles when he sees it's just a squirrel, not a feral dog or some furry demon. And it is then that the article in the paper under his head catches his eye.

Just a few lines about a shooting at a Shell garage upcountry. That two men were fatally shot. And that an as-yet-unidentified woman survived. The men had been shot in the head. Her Pajero had gone up in flames, making it hard for police to identify her. Police have yet to discover the reason for the shooting as the till had not been robbed.

Jabulani is over the moon that he does not, however obliquely, have her blood on his hands.

And yet, another afternoon of being snubbed and scorned taps his euphoria dry. Now he's told *so sorry* with a pitying smile, now he's told to *voetsek!*

A smug hissing through snarled lips: *Voetsek!* The thing you shout at gadfly dogs.

He walks though the cobbled Malay Quarter of houses painted in lurid colours on crazily slanting streets. The happy houses laugh at a world otherwise so dull and flat. Chirping women in vivid head cloths remind him of macaws. All white-framed doors and windows shut and shuttered to him. Through the door of a mosque he sees men dipping white beards to the floor. They are all aligned, like sheep in the wind.

At dusk Jabulani walks downhill to sit like a starved, jaded Buddha on the harbour wall.

Robben Island glows in the dusking orange. And a fevered sea flings up kelp offerings. Yet he feels shot down. All hollowed out.

29

Hermanus. After dusk.

A half-moon hangs in the frangipani in front of Lotte's house. Fairy lights do indeed dance in the sea wind. Lotte's sitting in a lotus mode on a Bali sofa, her feet folded up under her. Johnny Clegg is singing that song on the hi-fi about a crocodile in the river and sharks in the sea:

It's a cruel crazy beautiful world . . .

Al and a few other guys stand around the fire in Bermudas. There's something tribal about it. Al's unwittingly tapping out the beat of the song with his tongs on an empty beer bottle.

The guys are immersed in deep dialogue: Do you stack firewood in a wigwam V or Jenga style? Do you spice a T-bone beforehand or just salt it on the fire? Do you uncoil the *boerewors* or not? If not, do you spike it with a kebab stick to keep it coiled? Do you cook fish in tinfoil or char the skin?

– Folk who cook on gas are *moffies*, tunes one dude forever *whirring* the wheel of his Zippo.

The gas fares far, like a lizard's yellow tongue.

Haha-ing and clinking of beer bottles confirm this universal axiom. Gas = *moffie*.

– I heard in America they cook hamburgers on the *braai*, says another.

The guys shake their heads and hiss *jissus* at the craziness of America.

Lotte unwinds from her lotus mode to tip wine from a bottle into the glasses of other lolling, murmuring girls.

Guys around the fire. Girls further away. It has always been this way.

I hover on the fringe of the guys, wishing I had the guts to just drift over to the sipping, fanning girls. Her being so near puts all my senses on edge. Through the muddling of male voices I hear the shuffling of frangipani leaves in the wind, the yips of distant dogs, the lilting cadences of her limpid voice. I imagine I can filter out all the macho guys to hear whales sing their mellow sorrows. And that I can see the world curving towards the horizon.

– One cool thing about this new South Africa is you no longer have to fear the ANC blowing you to hell and gone, remarks Al.

– And you no longer have to check out on TV them chucking a tyre over a man's head and lighting him up, Zippo Dude tunes.

He apes the shuddering dance of a man burnt in the townships as an informer.

– That's uncool, scolds Al. Find another gig if you want to act like an asshole.

– Hey, chill, man, Zippo Dude whines.

Then, to deflect the focus, he sounds me out:

– How do you feel about firelighters?

– Me? I haven't given it much thought.

He nods as if this underscores his instinctive view of me as some-how dodgy. Latently gay or Communist.

– The art of it is to get the fire to catch just using slivers of wood and newspaper, Al teaches.

– *Ja*. Firelighters is for pussies, says another.

Yet another tidy axiom.

– Hey. Fetch us another round of beer, Zippo Dude tunes me.

This is an apartheid tableau. White man commandeering a loi-tering coloured *boy* to do an odd job for him.

– You'll find beer in the bathtub, says Al. Ta for the favour, hey.

I weave through the girls on the veranda. Lotte's caught up in dialogue with a girl.

– They found out it's not aliens, you see. It's kangaroos high on poppy. Their hopping forms those circles in the rye.

I wish to hover there, hanging on her words, staring at the ghost lips on the rim of her wine glass, but another girl frowns at me for eavesdropping.

I kick off my All Stars and go barefoot over cool marble floors through a lounge of white sofas and rippling white curtains. Riot-ous oil paintings hang unframed and raw on the stark white walls. Hers? I sense so.

The bathtub is full of ice cubes and floating, chilling bottles of beer and cider. I fish out a few Windhoeks and a Savanna Light for me.

As I go by the girls again, Lotte sees me.

– Oh, there you are.

Her hand beckons me over like a good-luck cat in a Chinese shop. My heart tap-dances.

– Girls, this is Jerusalem, the guitar guy I told you about.

Muted, in-cahoots smiles. I sense she didn't merely allude to my guitar.

– Come, Lotte cajoles, play for us.

– Oh yes, do, the girls chorus.

– I was sent to fetch beer.

– Oh, let them get their own beer.

I put down the beers and unzip my guitar.

I drop a pick and Lotte picks it up off the tiles. It's always tricky peeling a pick up off a flat floor. I don't let the nails on my picking hand get long, like some guitarists or some old Chinese men who see a spiralling fingernail as a measure of their unfazed aura. I catch a peek of her breasts as she bends down. My cheeks fizz and I focus on tuning the strings.

She smiles a slow, sly smile as she hands me the pick. As if she felt my eyes on her hidden skin. Then she glides over to the hi-fi and kills the music.

Al, perhaps pissed off that a girl's fiddling with his hi-fi, shakes the dregs of his beer over the sizzling *boerewors*.

I tentatively finger a few strings and key down E.

– What do you want me to play?

– Play something lyrical.

– Lyrical?

I begin to play *Moonshadow*.

The girls swing feet and hum-sing along.

Zippo Dude huffs over to pick up the beers. He smirks at me when he sees I am a Savanna boy. Evidently Savanna Light's pussy juice.

He clanks the beer bottles to *sabo* the song. Lotte glares at him.

After the song Zippo Dude chucks a coin at my feet.

– Hey Cat, play us another.

He laughs at his joke until Al jabs his hot tongs at him.

— You flipping *craaazy*? yelps Zippo Dude. You want to brand me for life?

I pocket the coin and play on.

Folk drop by until the yard is thrumming and the sound of my strumming is lost. Al switches to Santana on the hi-fi. I'm off the hook.

Lotte slides folded money into my jeans' ass-pocket. She begs me to stay longer.

And not all the folk are shallow and crass. A few are cool. There's a woman doctor who sees hope for curbing HIV after Mandela's 46664 concert in Cape Town. And then there's this zany bald actor called Sjaka (a white Sjaka?!).

And yet I am only half-tuned into dialogue. The recurring riff in my mind is: Who am I, a stranger and a coloured, to waltz into her white world?

Joints glow and float from finger to finger. I toke too and the world warps weirdly. The moon is a Chinese lantern. The stars are scattered fireflies. A hosepipe snakes through the frangipani to spit water at girls till their dresses echo their skin and their nipples jut.

And Lotte spins in slow-mo as fairy lights cast psychedelic tints over her.

I lose her for a long time, then somehow I am on the sofa beside her. In front of a covey of her girlfriends, I beg her to slide off her diamond ring. It blinks in my palm. Then I form a fist and when I unfurl my fingers again there's just a frangipani flower instead. Other girls go *oooh* and she smiles tenuously. She's half enchanted, half scared I may pinch the ring.

Sometime around midnight a random girl rubs champagne in my hair.

Sometime way after midnight the frangipani falls with one ma- cho swing of a long-bladed *panga*. Lotte sobs and Al begs her not to be so theatrical.

The frangipani is hauled into the house and stood up in a deep Chinese vase. Boys cajole girls to peel off their panties and hang them up in it. One girl fleetingly moons the boys. They howl like wolves.

Now panties hang from the frangipani like Tibetan prayer flags.

Lotte runs out of the yard onto the sea path. No one notices as they are all too caught up in grooving to an old Toto song. The fact that all the girls are nude under their skirts keys up the vibe and the boys jam hard.

I recall Zero dancing years ago in Amsterdam with such gusto that he went through the floorboards like Rumpelstiltskin.

I snatch up my guitar and follow Lotte.

She runs barefoot along the path to the old harbour, her white dress flapping in the cold sea wind.

I catch up with her on the old harbour slipway.

– I'm sorry about your frangipani.

She wipes liquid from her eyes with her palms.

– It was planted when I was born. Just a few days ago it bore oranges out of the blue . . .

The wind, whistling in the hollow of my guitar, echoes my lust for her.

– . . . and I sense it had something to do with you.

– Lotte, I fell for you the moment I saw you under a haze of flapping gulls. I love a myriad things about you: the way your soles peel so languidly, so subtly off the cool tiles of your veranda, the way you fold your feet up under you so felinely. I love the slant of your eyebrows, like wind-bent dune grass. And I love the whisper of freckles on your cheeks.

She stares out to sea and nibbles the skin of her lower lip. I can tell she's vacillating, as if she's teetering on a high wire. Then she swings her head to face me.

– Kiss me, before I change my mind.

– And Al?

– He's a sweet guy, but he'd kill you with his bare hands if he caught you.

This just proves old Hunter's right as a southern right. Things can get hazardous.

I kiss the silky skin under her ear. I comb my fingers through her hair and float my lips over her forehead, then kiss her fluttering eyelids.

The sea riots against the barricade of the harbour wall. A shooting star falls like a shot flare. A distant baboon or freak dog barks at that lantern of a moon.

My cock yearns hard for pink nirvana.

I kiss her lips. Our tongue tips tango viscously.

We huddle down in the lee of the harbour wall on my rugby jersey. I am bare to my jeans.

Moonfleet stalks over to sniff us. Lotte giggles at the tickle of his whiskers on her skin. Then he curls into the curve of my guitar.

She draws my hand under her dress. I feel the cold swell of her breasts under my palm. Her voice falls a few octaves to become sandy in my ear.

– You smell of champagne, she says.

She lays herself out flat before me.

I'm aware this may be a warped revenge for the felling of her frangipani rather than any deep love for me, yet I lingeringly lick her slightly salty cowrie shell. I am an awed artist tentatively painting the face of a Buddha.

30

Long street, Cape Town.

Yet another day of stalking his fortune and eluding Ghost Cowboy.

Crook hand hidden in his pocket, Jabulani doffs his hat to fellow Zimbabwean interlopers with his good hand. He licks the smell of coffee out of the air. His bones click and catch after another night in the paper bin in a courtyard behind a bookshop.

He'd put a coin under the lid to let a draft in: a fusion of sewer and gas and rat and rotting fruit. A gecko slid through the crack and skittered elusively among the scrap paper and flat boxes. He dreamed it was rats in the roof again and that he was in Thokozile's arms. He was so sublimely happy in his dream that when a dog toppled a reeking bin at dawn, Jabulani swung his lid up to curse him. His hand found a Canon ink cartridge and he flung it. It hit a wall, spitting out flecks of magenta. Then he fell into yet another dream: this time of his old cat swinging from a string. His cry yanked him out of this fitful dream, scattering gulls that haggled like fishwives over spilt junk.

Now the jangle of church bells in his ears reminds him of his school in Bulawayo.

In his mind he sees Panganai and Tendai in school, hiding their scabby shoes under their desks, borrowing paper from others, dodging questions about their father. Then he sees Thokozile scavenging for their tuck.

Just as something wild in him wants to howl against the injustice of things in this world, a pigeon lands on his head. He interprets this as yet another good omen.

Then the pigeon flaps away to land on the roof of an old green Benz.

He filches a newspaper and a stained, floppy banana out of a bin. He stands in a shaft of sun in front of a bookshop reading the paper and letting the fragrant banana melt on his tongue. He reads stories of rage and blood shot through with the cocky call of the pigeon.

He feels snide eyes glide over him as fancy folk go by. A man in white flip-flops eating a dangling-skinned banana like a monkey, yet reading the *Cape Times* as if he has a job at a desk in one of the tall buildings that scratch the sky overhead.

To avoid sliding into gloom he drops the banana skin (hoping one of the smug men in fine flannels will wipe out) and focuses on the pigeon again. This comical, moth-eaten bird croons as if he's the Bono of birds. You can tell he thinks he's the thing all girl birds dream of.

He hears glass clink and looks up from the paper to see a man in a parrot-vivid Hawaiian shirt and snakeskin boots putting a box of whisky into the boot of his Benz.

The pigeon flies off.

His eyes are about to revert to the newspaper when he sees, out the corner of his eye, the sun glint off the blade of a knife. Somehow time warps out like a tape left too long in the sun. Jabulani sees a hand follow that blade out of shadow.

The wind tugs at the falling newspaper.

By the time the newspaper lands, Jabulani's dived the knife-guy down. He hits him low and hard.

The knife spins through the air.

A head bangs into a hubcap.

Zero jumps at this cymbal *boom*. He draws his Colt 45 and swings it wildly.

A woman drops to the pavement, wailing: *No shooooot!*

Then Zero sees all. Him on the pavement at his feet. Out cold. Blood slipping from a slit in his head. And him with white flip-flops and one hand bound up like a boxer's.

Zero pockets his cowboy gun and helps the now jibbering woman to her feet.

– Sorry, mother. Sorry.

His voice calms her fears. He puts money in her hands. She shuffles on, mumbling to her god.

Jabulani dusts off his shirt and studies his hand where the blood inks through the cloth again.

Zero flicks the knife-guy over with his foot.

Just a boy. Maybe as young as Jero.

His eyelids flutter. His finger dabs at the slit. Then his eyes pop out white as pool balls at the sight of the blood. Then he's gone all lopsided, skedaddling along on all fours like a darted monkey.

Zero laughs.

Jabulani's amazed.

– Why'd you let him go?

– Jail will just further fuck him up. And I'm not in the mood to put him in the boot. I need time to think this out.

His hands shake as he lights a Camel.

– I'm fazed, I tell you.

– You want one?

– Ta.

– I always thought there was a hoop of luck around me.

– Maybe I'm your luck.

In a café on Greenmarket Square:

ZERO: You saved my skin.

JABULANI: Forget it.

ZERO: You crazy? How can I forget the fact that I'd be gone if not for you?

He pans his eyes over the market as if to encompass all the things he'd be gone from.

ZERO: I want to help you. You have a job?

JABULANI: I'm looking for a job.

ZERO: You have papers?

JABULANI: No. Just my wits.

ZERO: That's tricky.

JABULANI: I'll find something.

ZERO: Where are you from?

JABULANI: Zimbabwe.

ZERO: I am sorry for you. Zimbabwe's fucked.

Just then a Zimbabwean drifts by, offering spindly giraffes to café-goers.

ZERO: It's a fucking diaspora.

Jabulani just nods at this bald fact.

ZERO: What kind of a job?

JABULANI: I'd love to teach again. But after being put down and spat at in this town, that feels like a pipe dream. I'd wax your Benz. I'd be your coffee boy. I'd carry your whisky crates. You see, I need to wire money to my family.

ZERO: So, you're a teacher.

JABULANI: English.

ZERO: English teachers are two a penny. It's hard to find a post. But perhaps I can rig a job for you somehow. The way you decked that guy! Your instincts are honed, man. From now on you'll shadow me wherever I go. And I'll deal with the paperwork.

JABULANI: I need a place to stay.

ZERO: I said *wherever*. My son's just shifted out. You can stay in his room. He loves books . . . books by South Americans and Indians.

JABULANI: And your wife?

ZERO: She no longer reads.

JABULANI: But how will she feel about having a stranger under her roof?

ZERO: You'll see.

A beat.

JABULANI: I wonder what he was after. That guy. Surely he wasn't going to lug a crate of whisky down the street after knifing you.

ZERO: I've seen stranger things.

31

Hermanus. Dawn.

Her curtains stay drawn. The fairy lights still flicker. Seagulls morbidly orbit her yard. Sparrows flutter and peck at fag ends and other debris on the grass and veranda. *Dassies* sulk warily in a tangled milkwood.

I stare at the stub of the *pangaed* frangipani, at the fallen, yellowing flowers.

In my mind I replay the moment when the moon plucked the pale face of the professor out of shadow. His eyes seemed not to see Lotte's moonlit breasts absurdly white against my cinnamon skin. Instead, he gazed out beyond us at the sea, his rival lover.

That luminous face floating over the harbour wall, it killed the magic. Lotte tugged on her panties and said she'd lost her head and this was crazy and she was sorry.

And then she was gone.

*   *   *

I run on along the path to the lagoon, staying away from the dunes to avoid being harassed by a gull. Ahead along the tideline I see a frenzy of gulls and crows hovering over some tatty flotsam. As I draw nearer, seagulls flap to the sky and crows hop away from the rags. The birds caw at me to piss off in bird lingo. Now I see a dead man tangled in the rags: the gurney hobo stranded like some sorry, shabby foetus. His eyes have been pecked out. Now it is my turn to hop away, gagging at the raw, thumb-deep holes.

The reek's so vile I tie my shirt over my mouth. I drag him over the tidal flats to the sugary sand of the dunes. Along the way I pick up mussel shells to hide his eyes. Then I dig into the sand with my hands. Seagulls loop overhead, yelling at me. Now and then a daring crow darts in to jab his beak at a bloody, bootless foot. I fling sand at the bird.

I pan the beach for folk. Just a silhouetted fisherman far down the beach. Otherwise deserted.

I rife through sodden, frayed pockets for a sign of who he is. All I find are strands of string, bits of sea glass, cowrie shells, rubber bands, a few coins and Zero's Bic. Amazingly it catches in the hollow of my hands. I pocket it. I shove him into the shallow hole. I lay my shirt over his haggard, scratched-up face and shift sand in and over him till he's gone. Then I wander along the beach to pick up stones to mark the place.

I feel tacky recycling *Redemption Song* from a film I saw of another death on a beach in Thailand. Yet it feels fitting somehow. That time it was a shark. A fluke, fictive demon shark that swam out of an author's head in a world where no man has ever been killed by a shark. I wonder, as I sing Marley's lyrics, how this hobo died. How he ended up so far from his gurney. He puffed up the way drowned men and spiky balloonfish do, but he may have been dead before the tide tugged him out. I wonder if it was just rocks that tore at his face. And I wonder why I want to bury him as I do, under a pyramid of stones (somehow Jewish, this), rather than call the police to zip him up in a bag and put him in a cold drawer.

I feel for the Bic in my pocket. Perhaps I am, after all, my father's son. Doing forbidden things underhand. But, in a land harrowed by crime, I have no faith in the police looking for long into the death of a random hobo.

I feel somehow dirty for just shoving the gurney hobo in a hole. I feel a hollow pang of longing for Lotte. And I feel too flat to barter. Instead I want to paint myself blue and hang a sign over my stall that reads: SICK ARAB. That'd do the trick. It did for Twain's Jim at a time when being a footloose black man was a crime.

To think that was America then, so long ago, and South Africa just yesterday.

But life goes on. I hear wind-flung seagull fugues, the bell of an ice-cream vendor, the whale crier's kelp horn. I smell smoke and kelp and dust and jasmine.

And blacks from all over Africa hang out behind the market stalls: plying their trade, whistling catcalls, laughing a dry music, jiving to a lackadaisical Lucky Dube, jingling coins in pockets, tapping out pithy texts, hiding from the sting of the sun, maybe dreaming of scratching the paint of some smug guy's Tuareg with a bottle top.

Now Buyu's coming towards me, whistling a tune into an empty bottle. And his jaunty step tells me he has something to report. He's tagged by the barefoot bus boys.

CRUEL CRAZY BEAUTIFUL WORLD

– The boys, they saw men dart a dog. That dog, he was licking out the empty mussels behind Quayside Cabin. They say the dog, he fell over . . . like this.

Buyu clicks his fingers.

– Then the men, they put him in a Land Rover.

– You saw this with your own eyes?

The boys nod. They sheepishly scratch sandpapery soles against shins. They find it hard to hide their smiles, sensing this info is gold dust to me.

Their chief, donning his Kangol hat, steps forward.

– That dog was one of the dogs wanting the Kentucky bones. You remember him? He had that stand-up hair on his spine.

A Rhodesian? I just remember there being a few begging curs.

– That Land Rover was a white Freelander. On the door was painted a black shark head. The mouth of the shark was like this.

He gapes his jaws wide to flash radiant teeth.

I am amazed again at street boys having such white teeth, just as I am amazed by the miracle of shanty folk wearing flawlessly white shirts amid the dust and chaos.

I recall seeing this shark-head icon in Hermanus.

– Do you know the company?

– They based in Gansbaai, tunes the Kangol boy.

– Cage-diving tours?

– *Ja.* White shark.

I have read about how they lure sharks for tourists with a bait of crushed sardines that they call *chum.* It bleeds a slick that sharks can smell a mile away.

Hunter chirps:

– But why would they dart a dog?

The Kangol boy doffs his hat to her.

– Now that is a mystery, ma'am.

He says each word tidily, as if talking to his teacher. And yet I wonder if he ever sat in a classroom.

Out of the corner of my eye I catch sight of iguana eyes gazing at me all level and unblinking out of a bald head. Phoenix. He's sitting on the veranda of the Fisherman's Cottage in his trademark pink Lacoste, under a lean-to roof. He lifts a flask to tell me *cheers*.

– Keep an eye on things for me, I tell Buyu.

I drift over. He's juggling his Chinese Baoding balls in his left hand.

– Hey, Phoenix. My old man send you?

– I had to pick up *perlemoen* and crayfish in Hawston. He sent this for you.

I unflap the wine box. Brimful of geckos and seahorses and other beaded things.

– Cheers.

– You surviving?

– I am. I have money for him. In my flat.

– I'll pick it up another time. I have to head out. Got a job in Sea Point at dusk.

– Time for a drink?

– Always. I put in an order for a Windhoek for you. That cool?

– Ta. What's in that flask? Coffee?

– A blend. Ginger and *buchu*.

Buchu is a kind of *fynbos*. The Hottentots brewed a medicine from it. The things folk put faith in in South Africa. Zulus glug seawater as a panacea. My mother puts peppercorns along sills to scare off ants.

I do not ask if the restaurant minds him sipping his backyard brew. They'd never hassle Phoenix.

I snatch a wire shark out the box and peck at his fingers.

He smiles. Not just one of his curbed, corner smiles. It feels good to conjure a toothy smile from Phoenix. Some of that hard-core husk is an act.

– Still reading your Freud?

– Am. It goes deep. Folk doubt him now. But it's a fact you can't rub out. At the end of the day all man's antics derive from lust.

So how's running a guy down with a taxi sexual? No doubt he'd tell me this was just a human version of buck butting heads over a mate. Some such oblique logic. And yet I feel I am on too shaky a footing now to refute Freud. There's not a note I play, hardly a thought I think that's not tinged by my lust for Lotte.

The waiter hands me my Windhoek Lager. I have to snatch the bottle before he pours it into a glass.

– Sorry, says the waiter.

– No. I'm sorry. It's just a quirk. I'm funny when it comes to beer.

Phoenix arcs a brow as if to say: *Not just beer.*

I love to drink beer out of the bottle. It has lingered in the bottle, travelled in the bottle, and it smokes its long-capped soul from the bottle when you flip off the lid. It feels crass to decant it into a random glass with hints of soap scent and cloth lint. It can tip my mood if I don't catch a waiter in time.

The waiter smiles forgiving teeth at me. Then he turns to serve a guy whose crow is pecking peanuts from his hand. The waiter's unfazed by the bird. I wonder what kind of animal you'd have to have in tow to spook folk. A crocodile, maybe?

– What kind of job you got in Sea Point?

– I'd rather not tell.

– What's Zero's caper this time? Gambling? Whoring? Hawking pirate films?

– You do your old man an injustice. He's not your run-of-the-mill man. And he loves you.

– He's an asshole to my mother.

– Your mother's been tuned into another frequency ever since . . .

A hiatus. My head goes hazy.

Phoenix swigs down a glug of his brew, then darts his eyes at me.

– Perhaps he acts like an asshole to allay the pain.

I gaze out at the market.

– Sometimes I feel like killing him.

Another lull. Market stalls sway as if they are boats moored in a harbour. Canvas canopies flap in the wind. The posse of bus boys mills in front of my stall. Buyu, all peppy and pop-eyed, is reeling off a story animated by a windmilling of his hands and a hopping from foot to foot. The bus boys laugh at his antics.

– Who's that boy?

– That's Buyu. He's Tanzanian. I was out riding this Vespa my old man bartered for me. I flipped him into a gully.

– Lucky.

A beat: ?

Then I cotton on.

– *Ja*. Lucky he survived. Just don't tell my old man.

– So now you're mollycoddling him.

– I'm not. I hired him. He earns a cut.

– Just a few days ago you sat at your desk dreaming and writing poems instead of your thesis . . . and now you are hiring and spinning out the jargon.

For one who has freeloaded for years, he's rather too cynical about my abandoned thesis. Somehow he earns his keep just by shadowing my father and shifting a few boxes to and fro.

I see my father's Benz in the lot. The sun beats it.

– How do the crayfish handle the sun?

– Bundled in wet newspaper.

I think of their fate. A ride in a hot boot. Then they go under cold tap water. It's the lack of salt that kills them. Just as I imagined the lack of bar jazz and arthouse movies in this town would kill me. Turns out I survive just fine, jazzless and film-free. There's jazz in the sounds of the market. And now a film's looping in my mind: a film of Lotte all nude and moon-pallid. It's the thought of her falling through my fingers that kills me.

He puts down the flask and fishes something out of his pocket.

– This is from your old man. He wants you to have it. And he says to tell you there's a guy staying in your room.

– Who?

– A Zimbabwean. He saved your old man's life yesterday. Some mad boy wanted to stab him in Long Street.

My heart beats an iambic *da-dum, da-dum*. The market blurs.

I hear the *zen* balls clink as Phoenix loses focus. He musses up my hair with his free hand.

– Be cool. He's unscratched. Ironic though. He seldom heads out alone nowadays.

The gift is a girl carved out of ivory. I feel ambivalent about having it. She's beautiful but maybe an elephant was shot for it. I've often taken her out of his desk drawer and held her, cool in my palm. He once told me it's walrus and that you can tell from the cracks, but somehow I doubt it. She's taboo but too beautiful to burn the way they burn the tusks of culled elephant in this country.

I put her in my pocket. I hear the Bic head clink against the ivory. I shift her to my other pocket.

Then I draw a shark's head on a napkin.

– You recognise this logo?

– That's a Gansbaai crew.

– Stray dogs have been vanishing in this town. The boys in front of my stall saw men dart a dog, then load it in a Freelander bearing this logo.

– There's strange shit going down nowadays. I'd check it out but I got another job after Sea Point. Up in Bloem.

– And not just strays. An old priest lost his deaf old dog. The dog may be dead by now. I think I'll go out on my Vespa.

– You don't want to piss off Gansbaai boys. That place has a long history of pirating. And don't be fooled by their skin colour. They may be whiteys but they'll cut you.

He pencils figures on a till slip.

– My cell. You call if you ever need a hand.

He signals for the waiter.

– Where you from?

– Me? I'm from Zimbabwe.

– Bulawayo?

– Yessir.

– What did you do before?

– I was a teacher.

I hear the Baoding balls clink, intimating that Phoenix is slightly fazed.

– I hope your country heals, he tells the waiter.

Phoenix folds up a crazy tip.

The Zimbabwean goes with a skip in his heels.

– That's weird, Phoenix says to me. Not just a teacher calling *me* sir . . . but that guy I was telling you of, the one who saved your father . . .

He pockets the Baoding balls and hooks out the Benz key.

– . . . he's a teacher too. You see?

He says this as if it is the clinching evidence for his theory of the world.

I gulp down the rest of my Windhoek.

He stands and I stand too to shake his hand. It's not just the thing my father taught me to do. Phoenix has an aura that yanks you to your feet.

I stay on his heels to the end of the market square and then hang there (where the fruit seller's juggling his oranges) as he winds through the parked motorcars to Zero's Benz. He winds down all the windows to let the cool sea wind blow through. He points two fingers at his eyes telling me to look, then signals out to sea. My eyes scan the sea. I see the convex hull of a whale's spine. Her blow fades to a mist, then vanishes against the blue.

I feel a keen, primal thrill. I run down to the low white viewing wall between tarmac and sea. I lean out over the gaping drop to the old harbour below. I see the professor standing on the harbour wall. The whale flips up its fluke as if bidding the professor hallo. The professor swivels his head and squints up (at me?) before sinking into his deckchair again. I feel he was mocking me: *Convex hull? Why can't you see the world without turning it into a metaphor?*

Only now does the whale crier's horn sound and tourists give up their place in the queue in front of a pink ice-cream van, leave off their curio hunting in the market, and abandon their fish and chips in the Burgundy to flock to the viewing wall.

I turn to wave goodbye to Phoenix. But he's gone.

I feel jilted amid this circus of foreign jabbering.

32

Sea Point, Cape Town. Dusk.

On the beachfront a band of wheezing, floppy-jowled old men in deckchairs blow a slow, slurred Dixie tune. A madman conducts with a frenetic chopstick. One lone vampire tooth juts randomly out of his jaw.

Zero, Canada Dry and Dove Bait go reservoir-dog-style over the road: their feet swing all loose and jazzy.

Jabulani lags a few beats behind, like the old men falling behind the pace tapped out by the vampire.

Then Phoenix follows after, his eyes panning for unforeseen flak.

Outside the door a beggar jingles coins in a tin. The coins sing: *Where do carp dart? Where do carp dart?*

Zero digs his hands into his pockets and drops a coin into the tin.

The beggar foretells a myriad virgins for Zero as if he's on a *jihad*. Zero laughs. And flips him another coin.

In the dim hallway a whore pouts gaudy lips and flashes a secret snatch of skirt skin.

Dove Bait lapses into a charmed daze.

Zero pinches his ear.

— Focus, man. You'll get us shot if your eyes detour.

The lift smells of piss and Jeyes Fluid. Zero holds the lift till Phoenix catches up. Phoenix draws an Uzi out of his kit bag. Compared to this stubby spitfire-demon of a gun, Zero's Colt is just a popgun.

— No shooting to kill, Zero intones. We go in. We teach them a lesson. We let them feel pain but survive. If they die, they learn zilch.

Dove Bait nods in awe of Zero's profound logic.

Canada Dry jokes:

— Yes, sir. May I wipe off the blackboard after class, sir?

— But this is radical. There has to be another way, Jabulani pleads.

— Teacherman, what *they* do is radical, tunes Zero. This is not just slitting a fish and flinging it into a pan while its heart's still beating. This is not just cooping a dog in a birdcage or hacking the fin off a shark for soup. Monkeys are just a notch away from being *human*.

His thumb and finger, two inches from Jabulani's nose, measure out that notch.

— But to shoot . . .

— This is the way to deal with monkey-gobblers.

— Why not call the police?

Canada Dry and Dove Bait laugh and shake their heads as if this is a damn good joke.

— We have to take the law into our own hands. It's a war out there and the police are as outfooted as the Americans in Nam.

– But it's not your war. What has this to do with you? With your wife or your son?

– When they hurt an animal or a child, they hurt me. I feel it in my bones. So it is my war. You see?

He hands Jabulani a handgun.

– I've never had a gun in my hand. I'm against violence.

Jabulani does not confess to his bid to kill a dazed sheep with a stone.

– I have always told my students . . .

– You and Gandhi. And they shot him. But Mandela gave his nod to violence when there was no other way. And unfortunately, there are men who understand just this one language.

The *pinging* of the lift ends the dialogue. Again Jabulani hangs a few yards behind.

Zero halts in front of door number 113 and signals like a Nam jarhead for Jabulani to catch up.

Beyond the door they hear men laughing and joking in a sing-songy foreign lingo.

Over the lintel a gecko eyes a moth's frenzied orbiting of a light bulb.

Zero nods at Canada Dry and Canada Dry back-pedals a few steps. Zero and Dove Bait draw their pistols from their pockets. Phoenix levels his Uzi.

The gecko zips after the moth. Moth wings flicker from his gob.

Canada hurls himself at the door like a rugby forward bent on barging his way over the try line. The door cracks and Canada Dry falls into the next filmic shot.

– This jig is up, yells Zero.

He swings his Colt as if he's a marine on camera.

Eyes gape, gobs call out to pagan gods, hands flutter haphazardly as bullets sing over the round table with that gory thing at the hub.

A monkey-gobbler draws a Black Star pistol and aims at Jabulani. Jabulani puts up his hands.

Zero shoots that monkey-gobbler in the collarbone. The Black Star spins out of his hands and blood spits like gust-flung dandelion darts.

Canada Dry, still down on the floor, stalks after the fallen Black Star.

The shot monkey-gobbler sinks to his knees.

Canada Dry's stoked with gun: *Waha!* Chinese pistol!

Another monkey-gobbler slides a tinted glass door ajar and hops onto the balcony wall.

There's a hiatus as all characters freeze (Jabulani's hands still up in the air). The soundtrack goes dead. There's an unscripted camaraderie to their staring at that comical figure see-sawing on the wall.

Then he's gone and they all flinch for the clichéd silver-screen yowl:

Yet the man falls soundlessly.

The most curious thing about this silence is that the scalped monkey (surrounded by half a dozen monkey-gobblers) is still thinking with the brain they were about to spoon out of his skull and he sends an unworldly whine into it.

And Jabulani's hands fall and his spine folds as his mind fades to black.

33

Hermanus old harbour. Just after dusk.

The professor is dozing on a deckchair under a sun-faded beach umbrella on the wall of the old harbour. He has guyed the umbrella down to stones with fraying string. The dog-eared paperback in his hands has lost its cover: either a short book or a torn-out sliver of a longer book.

Moonfleet's barks wake him.

He scowls at me.

– You.

– Yes. That a novella you reading?

– Honed and bare-boned.

– Hemingway?

– Camus. *The Outsider.*

– I thought he wrote *The Stranger*.

– Same book.

– That's a loophole in my reading.

– Gist is: white guy shoots an Arab.

I recall being sent to a fancy *white* school in Cape Town when we came from Amsterdam. On paper apartheid had been dead for two years (since Mandela was freed in 1990), but the other boys gawped at me. To them I was an alien. My name did not conform. They had no pigeonhole in their head for a half Jew, half Muslim. In the schoolyard they called me *dirty Arab*. On the athletics track I lapped them. I licked them hollow and mute. But in the schoolyard the baiting went on for another two years, until Mandela was voted in.

– So why'd he shoot that Arab. Revenge?

– Not revenge. Nor any other kind of rancour. He hated no one. And he loved no one. That Arab just happened to be on the beach at the same time.

– That's hardly a crime.

– Was for dark folk in South Africa, not long ago.

– So he just shot him in cold blood?

– No. The sun fucked with his head.

– You can't blame the sun.

He stares out beyond me and I realise he's remembering again the way the sea ravaged his wife.

I think I've lost him, but then he says:

– Was it not the sun that illuminated that girl for you?

I am stumped by this. He saw me see her. How does he travel unseen along the path? Swing through the milkwood *bundu* like some kind of spider monkey?

– I'd have fallen for her anyway.

– She's just a girl. The sun tricked you.

– She's beautiful. Not in the fake way of flick girls, but somehow innately beautiful.

– You love that word. *Beautiful*. A beautiful dog. A beautiful girl. What is beautiful? What are your yardsticks? Is all life not beautiful? Was that Zimbabwean they killed not beautiful? Is my sun-wizened face not beautiful? Why do you need to label things? This is good. This is evil. This is beautiful. This is not.

– But you must see that she's an angel. Her skin's flawless.

I just so happen to have the milky, unsunned skin of her breasts in mind.

He laughs.

– And her eyes are magic. They're this sublime, lagoony blue-green. I think you'd call it viridian.

– Viridian's more green than blue. You more Arab than Jew?

– My father's half Malay, half Cuban. My mother's a Jew.

I drift in reverie. Recall the day Miriam fired Zero's Colt to scare baboons from a picnic we had on Noordhoek beach. The shot spooked a horse that threw its rider. And I thought: This could never happen in Amsterdam.

– All I see is a girl. All I see is a man dead. Why call her an angel? Why call him a refugee?

This old professor must have left his students reeling. I want to tell him you have to label things to get by . . . but I'd sound like my old man, wouldn't I? Yet it's hard to deny labels are handy. My father's *coloured*. So am I. Just less so, if such a thing can be measured.

I recall learning in school that a crude yardstick in the old Cape for finding out if a man was coloured was to put a pencil in his hair. If he shook his head and it fell out, he wasn't.

– So they condemned him, then? The guy who shot the Arab?

– They condemned him, in the end, for not crying when his mother died. And for putting milk in his coffee. That's the fucked-up thing about this world. They damn you for random, irrelevant things. For the tint of your skin. For being gay. For being Zimbabwean.

I just stand there wondering if I will cry at my mother's funeral.

34

Cape town. Night.

Jabulani studies the things in Jerusalem's room. A pansy-shell fossil. A cricket bat. An old guitar, the rim sheen worn away by years of strumming. A row of books: Steinbeck's *Of Mice and Men*, Camus's *The Stranger* (no sign of him having read it), Hemingway's *The Old Man and the Sea* (a first printing from 1954 with a guineafowl feather tucked in it), Paton's *Cry, the Beloved Country* (an old copy pinched from a school library), Mda's *Ways of Dying* (pages warped from falling into liquid . . . perhaps the pool, or the sea) and (inevitably) Coetzee's *Disgrace* (subtle cracks of the spine).

No books by South Americans or Indians. Maybe he took them along to that town by the sea. He finds it curious that the books are free of annotations . . . just yellowed by time and perfumed with dust.

Zero, Canada Dry, Dove Bait and Jabulani study a map on the kitchen table. An array of glasses tells the story of a long night.

Phoenix gazes out the window at Miriam dancing a *t'ai chi* waltz in the moonlight. She weaves among her colony of gnomes with an unseen wind-lover. The gnomes smile at his fiddling with her skirt. They smile at the smile he conjures from her lips. They smile at the yellow ghost snake (the memory of a hosepipe) winding through the yard to the empty pool.

– The girls get caught by the *gumagumas* on the border.

Zero's finger travels south from Limpopo province to Bloemfontein in the old Orange Free State.

– Then they end up in a brothel, or get sold as maids. There's no register of such a girl. She can vanish without the world blinking an eyelid.

He blows through his lips. *Poof.*

– My man in Polokwane took these shots.

He scatters photos of a girl bundled into a Cherokee.

– Just yesterday afternoon. Fake licence. But check this out.

Zero holds up a blurred shot he'd radically zoomed into. Part of a blurred garage logo: TOLK-.

– Folk? Jabulani wonders.

– No. *Tolk.*

– Turns out there's just one garage beginning with Tolk – in this country. Tolkien Jeeps in Bloemfontein. And there's just two Jeep Cherokees on their books. One belongs to a butcher. The other to a farmer. One of them's going down. I figure it's the farmer. The butcher shop's in downtown Bloem. Too tricky to hide a girl. Besides, the butcher's never the evil guy in a crime novel. Too tacky.

They all laugh, other than Jabulani and Phoenix.

– So this too is your war? Jabulani taunts.

– You're learning, teacher, Zero laughs.

He focuses on the map again.

– I have to figure out how to find this farm.

Jabulani studies the lurid pink scar in the V of his hand.

– What about the story I told you guys? What about Ghost Cowboy and Jonas and that girl on the marijuana farm?

– I have to get this girl out. We go tonight. Then we'll figure out how to catch your cowboy ghost. And we'll find that ox-head on a post.

– What post? Dove Bait wonders.

– You tell, Zero nods to Jabulani.

– You see, the skull of an ox impaled on a pole marks the dirt road to the marijuana farm where they held me captive. There's no other sign.

Jabulani wonders if she's surviving, the girl he howled at. He wonders if another Zimbabwean has had his corpse flipped from the flatbed of the truck into the croc pond. He wonders if they still play football at dusk and if old Jonas still *pangas* a watermelon to sweeten their bitter lot. And if he thinks Jabulani forgot.

He walks out into the moon-silvered yard. Miriam's cat zeroes in on him. She rubs her leopardy fur against his shins, as his cat did. He gathers this cat in his hands and combs his fingers through her hair. She stares turquoise eyes at him.

Miriam abandons her dance. Now she sees this hitherto unseen stranger through the eyes of her cat.

– You love cats, she murmurs.

– Never seen this kind.

– A Bengal. Foreign.

– Like me, Jabulani smiles.

– Where are you from?

– Zimbabwe.

– I am not scared of you.

– That's good. All I want is to earn money to send to my wife and children.

– You have children?

– A son and a daughter. Still at school. I gather you have a son.

– I had a daughter.

Jabulani feels as if he's walking along that high beam again.

– I am sorry for your loss . . . What happened to her?

She back-pedals, gathering her dress in a fist until it hardly covers her hips.

– Why?

– Sorry.

She spits out a rueful laugh and rocks on her heels. She winds her hair up with her free hand.

He lets the cat slide to the grass and enfolds her in his arms.

She flinches. After a time she lets her hair fall.

From the window Phoenix sees a dispersed Zimbabwean holding a pining Jew: two lonely, diasporic souls clutching at each other in a hard, spurning world.

35

Hermanus. After midnight.
Buyu and I walk along the cliff path to her house.

The sea is curiously calm.

There's a hint of indigo in the gull-less sky. And the moon hangs like a pearl from Scorpio's hooked tail.

That raw frangipani stump in her front yard is empirical evidence I did not dream her.

There's a risk folk will report seeing two dodgy characters loitering on a wall, but we sit on it anyway, all foot-swinging and tomcat-cocky.

I pluck my guitar. I see her shadow glide behind filmy white curtains. Then, for a long time, there's no hint of her.

Buyu lies down flat on the wall and stares up at the stars.

I play on till I conjure her shadow again. Now it stays and sinuously lilts. Lotte subtly swaying her hips to my music? Or just a slight breeze drifting along the curtains?

Buyu dozes off, his eyes white under slit lids, his feet jigging like a dreaming dog's.

Between tunes I hear an owl calling *hoo hoo*, the zither of mosquitoes and the snarl of Buyu's breath over the listless sighing of a low tide.

Now lights in the house go out. For a long time it's dark behind the curtains. I am about to abandon this futile serenading and to joggle Buyu awake when the curtains slide apart, just a few inches, maybe a foot.

Caught naked in the moonlight, she's an angel between two vast white wings.

Forgive me if this riles you, O Professor, but this is how I define beautiful.

36

Bloemfontein. Afternoon.

A mystic-green Benz coasts through the town.

Zero's drumming his palms on the rim of the wheel to the beat of a Midnight Oil song.

Phoenix rides shotgun, his face a stoic mask.

Canada Dry and Jabulani sit in the back of the Benz. Canada Dry spins a revolver on his finger. Now and then he aims at a random dog or a bird on a wire and goes *pow-pow, pow-pow!*

Dove Bait they left in Cape Town to keep an eye on Miriam and her rat-taunting cat and the happy-go-lucky gnomes. Besides, he'd lose his head around young girls.

Zero halts a block beyond the Cherokee butcher's shop. He goes in for *boerewors*.

The butcher is paring a sheep down to flat chops with a band-saw that now whines as it cuts through bone, now hums as it glides through flesh, now whines, now hums. He abandons his sawing, wipes blood off his hands.

– *Middag.*

– Afternoon. That's a cool jeep you got out front.

– *Ja.* There's few in these parts.

– Aha.

– You have a wish?

– *Boerewors.* Two coils.

– You want spicy?

– Spicy's good.

The butcher parcels the *boerewors* in Manila paper. He tallies up the cost with a pencil on the paper.

Zero hands over a few notes. The *tinging* of the till is a sound from Zero's youth. This place is a time warp. Yellow flypaper spiralling down from the roof. A standing steel fan swivelling and rattling. A *Scope* pin-up of a skinny white girl in a bikini flaunting fat tits. Johnny Cash singing on the radio.

There's no sign that this is post-apartheid South Africa, apart from a fading shot of a jubilant Mandela in a Springbok rugby shirt (rather uncoolly buttoned all the way up) after the Boks beat the All Blacks back in 1995 . . . just a year after freedom. And then the fact that he, a coloured, is being served without the butcher batting an eyelid.

– That game came down to the wire, hey? Zero remarks, nodding at the photo of Mandela

– *Ja.* You saw it?

– I was overseas. Saw it in an Irish pub in Amsterdam full of bloody *rooineks.* They all yelled for the All Blacks. No one was for us then, hey?

– *Ja.* The world was against us.

– When that ball flew through the posts, I tipped the rest of my beer over my head and went out onto the banks of the Amstel and danced a jig.

The butcher laughs.

– You wouldn't want to sell me that jeep of yours?

– No. But there's a farmer out at a farm called Jakkalspan. His jeep's all scarred and dented. I wonder where the hell he goes with that thing. Maybe he would sell.

– How can I find this farmer?

– Here. I'll draw the way out for you.

– You can't call him?

– He has no telephone. He's like one of those Indian kermits hiding away in a cave.

Zero smiles at his fumbling of *hermit*. He'll have to tell Jero. It'll kill him.

At a 7-Eleven they pick up buns and tomatoes.

Just beyond town they ride along a rutted road. They go past a fat-hipped woman with a baby cocooned against her spine and a plastic keg of water on her head.

Further on they go past a few zinc shanties huddling in the sketchy shade of a stand of bluegums. Colourful washing hangs out on barbed wire and smoke unspools from a fire. Boys play football barefoot with a tennis ball. Girls play a game akin to hopscotch, where they hop on one foot and hold their other foot by the heel. There's a paradoxical holiday mood, as if they are camping by the sea instead of along a dirt road.

One girl shoots through a hole in the wire at the sight of the Benz and runs in their dust wake. She has no hope of catching them, yet she runs as if a mad dog's on her heels.

Jabulani thinks: *Just a few days ago I was running hard and head-long as that girl.*

After half a mile Zero halts the Benz and winds down his window.

The girl now catches up, halts a few yards short, stares warily at them. There's no telling if folk will toss pennies or stones.

– You are fast, young girl, Zero tells her. You go on running like this you'll become a Zola Budd.

For her a Zola Budd's a taxi. She's never heard of the barefoot runner. But a taxi's a zoom-along thing, so she flashes dazzling teeth at Zero.

He holds out a note. She skips up to him and curtsies for the money.

– Stay well, girl.

– Go well, sir.

They go on, slowing at the sign of the farm they are looking for: Jakkalspan. Then they go on another mile or so until they find a bridge over a river. Zero parks the Benz under a bluegum.

They make a fire out of newspaper and driftwood down on the river sand. They cook the *boerewors* and put it on the buns with slices of tomato. They down Black Label beer from an icebox.

Jabulani and Canada Dry strip down to their jockeys and swim in the river.

Zero lies on his shirt and sings along to a song by Masekela about a woman floating through the marketplace like a butterfly. He thinks about Jero in the market in Hermanus. Phoenix told him Jero's cool. But he wonders how his life will pan out. He hopes having to hustle to survive will kill that fool dream of his of becoming a poet. He hopes he'll find a good girl who never goes cold on him. And he hopes, above all, Jero will never have to scatter the ashes of his child, the way he had to.

Jabulani and Canada Dry chuck a tennis ball to each other over the surface of the river. They dive and *whoop* like schoolboys until they both lie winded and worn out on the sand.

Jabulani rewinds the call he put through to Bulawayo from Ze-ro's telephone. He had to beg folk from over the road to call Tho-kozile. Their telephone had been cut off long ago. He'd heard them call her name. And then he'd heard her panting in his ear and he'd imagined her breath hot as a dog's on his skin. And he did not tell her about the marijuana farm or his being shot or about a falling monkey-gobbler. All he said was that he was in Cape Town and that it was beautiful beyond words and that he'd found a way to earn money doing odd jobs and would wire money for Christmas. She'd sobbed and he'd told her he loved her, that she was never out of his mind, and he'd vowed he'd come for them soon. He'd been stoic un-til he put the telephone down. And then he'd gone out in the dark and climbed down into the empty pool. He'd lain face flat on the pool floor. He'd felt the memory of the sun seep into his skin. He'd heard the dogs of the hood bark their tom-tom poetry at the moon. He'd felt his ribs would snap with the soul pain that bore down on him, splaying his feet and hands out. To bats hunting lamp-dazzled moths, he may have looked like a skydiver falling through a faded blue sky.

And the sandpapery tongue of a Bengal cat licking dry salt from his face had lured him to lift his eyes to the sight of Miriam dancing alone under the moon. Curiously, it felt like so long ago, like a déjà vu from another lifetime.

And now the falling sun is a flaming, tacky pink, just like the end of a cowboy flick.

37

Hermanus.
   Time blurs on her cool, white floor. A sketchy, sepia light is cast through the fat fingers of the cut frangipani. The sea, wind-warped, sings in my ears.

I felt guilty sending Buyu alone to the flat. But if he survived *gumagumas* and rabid dogs, then the path was not too risky: just a crabby professor and snakes to dodge.

He was all sparky in the market all day, hustling and skipping while I sipped sour black coffee.

Now, as my eyes pan along her paintings, they turn into film shots:

Drops of blood, spat like viscous Tabasco from the eyes of a mer-maid onto her breasts, travel down towards her belly button. But before they arrive a stray dog laps them up off her skin.

White pigeons fly out of a pussy (her?) and a fantasy animal (half hyena, half Tasmanian devil?) bares jagged fangs and catches them out of the sky with a long, lurid tongue.

A vulture dips its head into the carcass of a seal and bobs up all red-skulled and gleeful.

A shark glides below an unwitting, wingless girl swimming on the surface of a lagoon . . .

I avert my eyes to focus on her. I want to lose myself in her the way I got lost in the mind of García Márquez. I put my ear to the lee of her hipbone and hear bubbles gurgle below her skin. My cock goes hard as cuttlebone. I swivel her and hold her heels high. Her nude love-flower lurks shyly between folded petals. I kiss this flower until it blooms to fill out my palm.

I let her heels go and her knees fall akimbo to flare a hint of pink.

Just her, her bizarre paintings and a dying frangipani. No dog or cat. No flowers.

– How come you stay here all alone?

– My mother died a few years ago. My father's away. He's a professor at a university in New York. I see him during his long summer holidays. We go for long walks along the path and go to Quayside Cabin for whitebait. And Al I see on weekends. I'm not too lonely in between.

I skirt away from the topic of Al.

– And no flowers or cats?

– I want the freedom to walk out without anything dying. Sometimes I go to Cape Town for a few days on a whim and stay at in my father's flat in Hout Bay. You look down on the harbour. If the wind blows off the sea it reeks from all the fish killing. But the view's beautiful.

– I imagine the birds and *dassies* pine for you when you're gone.

– Perhaps. But they survive.

Will I? I wonder.

– Tell me about your paintings.

– I don't talk about my paintings. That'd be deciphering them for you . . . telling you how to look.

I'm scared of saying something uncool, so I just let her words float.

– But I'll tell you why I love hazardous art.

– Hazardous?

– Hazardous. It rents this kind of sharky, cavernous place in your head. Its edges are like some smoky vapour.

I glance at the painting of the shark: jaw unhooked and eyes coldly smug.

– And yet that's not it either. There isn't a language for it. It sounds crazy . . .

– No. Not crazy.

I snuff at the skin behind an ear foetal-folded and cool-rimmed. She sighs. Art is forgotten. And I sigh too, for I am in no mood to follow her into that sharky place now.

– This is a dream. You and me. A magical dream, yet there's no future for us. You see that, don't you? I don't want you hurting.

– Why just a dream? My dark skin?

– You crazy? I love the yummy colour of your skin: halfway between butternut and cinnamon. It's just that Al and I have a long history. I fell for him when I was still a schoolgirl and he was a student at Wits. It was so cool to cruise around Jozi in a convertible MG with this older guy who took me to arthouse films and hip bars.

She smiles, recalling perhaps a vision of a younger Lotte, wind-tousled and high on the whirl of a now-vanishing Johannesburg. To cruise around in a convertible these days is begging to be hijacked or shot through your Ray-Banned head.

– It's just that he no longer makes my blood fizz when he makes love to me.

I sulk.

– I just can't imagine him tuning into you the way I do. He doesn't seem the arthouse type.

– He saw the films for me. That's a measure of his love. He may seem a bit fuddy-duddy and old-line on the surface. But he's sharp, and honest to the bone. And he's never hurt me. This sounds shallow and crass, but he's made a lot of money and that frees us to travel the world, rather than feeling trapped on the edge of it. I want to paint the Taj Mahal and Uluru. I want to put up my paintings in London and New York. I want to hang out in Bali and die in Mexico.

It feels too tacky now to tell her I too want to see the world. It would sound borrowed and callow. Yet I sense I'd want to see it in another way to her. Just the music in the name of a town lures me. I have no defined plan to see any landmarks or to capture anything. I doubt I'd take photographs. I'd just want to drift maplessly through Malacca or Mandalay or Timbuktu or wherever and live the vibe and sip cold beers in dusty cafés and write poems or whatever fell into my head. I'd earn money as I went along by playing my guitar on street corners. (Another Zero mantra: *You'll never starve if you can play the guitar.*)

I wonder if Zero has money pocketed away or if the profits from his gigs just tide him over. Perhaps he rides an old Benz not just out of fondness for the square old box, but because he doesn't have the money to fork out for a Z3 or something jazzy. I may inherit the house in time . . . if Phoenix's old foes don't find him and burn it down. But that jaded, viewless house so far from the sea would hardly fetch a fortune.

– And me? I'm just a poor boy?

– Not just. You are absurdly beautiful.

I spit out half a laugh. Take note, O Professor.

– You play the guitar sublimely. And you have a way with words that drugs me. And yet . . .

– I see.

And I'd had the gall to imagine that if the stars aligned otherwise for us, or if a coin fell tails instead of heads, or if the moon tugged harder . . .

38

A farm somewhere just outside Bloemfontein.
Farmhouse lights burn yellow on a low hill a few miles ahead.
Zero cuts the headlights and they ride on by the light of the moon.
They abandon the Benz a mile or so from the house and go on by foot.

Two Isuzu pickups are parked in the yard. A boerboel dog hurtles towards them, rattling a deep bark from his canines.

Phoenix darts him down. He fondles the dog's ears as he slides into puzzled slumber.

They find the dirty, dented Cherokee in the garage. TOLK-. The telltale letters kill any doubts.

The door of the farmhouse is ajar.

There's a TV on (Paul Newman cycling a bicycle in circles) and muffled sounds from below.

They steal down dark cellar steps. Now they hear a whimpering, followed by men laughing. Phoenix goes ahead, lizardly stalking the light at the end of the steps.

A bottle of Old Brown sherry goes from hand to hand among three men. They stand around a crazed-eyed girl with a handkerchief balled in her mouth. She's on tiptoes, hands tied over her head to a hook in the roof. Her torn dress hangs like shed skin from her hips. Another girl, head hanging down, is tied to a bentwood chair in the corner. She's naked from head to foot.

The hardtack dulls the senses of the men, but the strung-up girl sees him and her eyes flare.

Phoenix signals to her to stay still. Then he puts the blowpipe to his lips.

A man smacks at his calf, thinking he's been stung by something waspy. His hand comes away filmed in blood. He's puzzled by the dart jutting out of his skin. By the time he cottons on and spins round, the world's tilting. He keels over.

Now Zero's on the bottom step, his Colt levelled at the other two men.

– Hands up, boys!

One man foolishly goes for a gun in his pocket. Zero puts a bullet into his foot.

The man howls as he hops on his unshot foot.

The third man dives behind the girl on the bentwood. Now he has a blade at her throat.

At that moment Jabulani peeps his head into the cellar. This freaks the guy out and blood slides subtly from under the blade.

– I'll kill her. I'll fucking . . .

Zero's bullet fillips his head. His blood fans out against a swastika flag on the wall.

Though the cut is just skin-deep the girl's voice is a crazy chorus of cicadas in a box.

*   *   *

Zero tugs the flag off the wall to throw over the corpse.

Then he pans a video camera, zooming in on the fear-ridden eyes of the whimpering, foot-shot farmer.

To him Zero jibes:

– You'll need a vivid imagination to come up with a story your wife falls for, hey?

The farmer lets out a sob.

– Not so cool now, hey?

Turns out, fortuitously, the darted guy's the Cherokee farmer. They tie him up with nylon ropes he'd used on the girl and bundle him into the boot of the Benz. He mumbles mumbo-jumbo. They stuff the spit-wet gag in his gob.

Zero tasks Phoenix and Jabulani with ferrying the girls to Cape Town on the back seat of the Cherokee.

Canada Dry shoots out the tyres of the Isuzu.

They let the one with the shot foot go. He hobbles along the dusty farm road after the fading red eyes of the Cherokee.

The only thing left alive in the farmyard is a dog under a sneeze-wood dreaming of catching ever-elusive moles. The spicy scent of the sneezewood pervades the world.

39

Hermanus market.

I wear a fake smile for Buyu and Hunter and the tourists. One gay guy from Berlin takes all my geckos for the walls of his Thai restaurant. Buyu jives and *yahoos*.

I ought to feel jazzed but I feel low and blue. I feel burdened by all the pain and injustice and sorrow that lingers below the mundane surface of things in this land.

I mosey over to the seafront for an ice-cream but the pink ice-cream van's gone. Instead I lie down flat on a rock in front of the Marine Hotel from where I can see the tidal pool far below. I want to zone out on the whizzing of grasshoppers and the hiss of the sea but am joggled by voices and hooting and a miasma of smoked fish and dust and dog dirt.

The spell Lotte cast over this town for me has worn off. The whales have gone. The sun glares down, fading colour out and warping things. Fish mysteriously float gut-up to the surface of the lagoon. A bloom of jellyfish plagues the bay. I catch a snatch of Buffalo Springfield (a line about a man and a gun) from a radio.

I've plucked angels and jinns from my guitar. I've fingered her nipples as fondly as an old man fingers rosary beads. I've followed the fringes of her angel feathers down to the foot of her spine, where they almost touch. I've murmured words into her ear till she arced her spine and rubbed her breasts against my ribs. I've felt her fingernails cut into my skin. I've cajoled a primal yell from between her teeth as her hips thrummed under me. And, in my midsummer folly, I thought I'd wooed her. But she'll not jilt him for me.

A lone, clown-bald hunchback on a bench blows his *vuvuzela* in monotoned farts. And between toots he forecasts a red tide.

I fling a stone at a lizard basking on a rock. It vanishes, just as I too will vanish. These rocks, this tidal pool, the old harbour wall, they will all survive long after my fleeting stay.

At noon I hand the stall over to Buyu. I'm proving to be as unfocused at trading as I was at studying.

On the way to the flat I stand and stare down at the old harbour far below. I feel a sweet vertiginous horror at the thought of my bones cracking on the cruel rocks. Just a step forward would end this fanciful dream of surviving as a poet in a world so ruthless and literal, would cure this ill-spent longing for Lotte. I wonder what makes me not jump. Some tenuous, muslin skin of sanity perhaps.

I step away from the taunting void and walk on.

I see a bare-scalped Xhosa girl alone at the tap, shifting a deep drum of water from knee to hip to shoulder. I give her a hand to put it on her head.

She mouths two shy syllables that sound like *O sir* to my ear but may be a word in her language.

She goes so lightly under her burden. Each lifting of a heel an *O*, each fall of bare-skinned sole a sighing, slurring *sir* in the dust of the churchyard.

I wonder how many miles she'll walk under her burden. I wonder if a boy has loved her yet.

Suddenly I feel ashamed of falling so foolishly into sorrow and gloom when there is such beauty in the world and folk will risk all to live longer under the sun.

I ride my Vespa out on the Maanskynbaai road again, past the lagoon where dead fish glint and a puzzled fish eagle calls from the bare white bones of a tree jutting out of the shallows, past where I wiped out and where a faded red bus dreams of London, past an obsidian-skinned whore in a curt skirt under a pink umbrella, past the road to the brewery, past a shabby ostrich, all the way out to Gansbaai till black, kelpy vines snake out of white dunes. The stringy survivors of a veld fire.

That girl lingers on in the stinging song of cicadas. Red lips beckoning from under a pink half-moon. She's proof of how radically things have changed in South Africa since Mandela was freed. Then sin and lack were well hidden and whores sold skin in dim alleys by the dockyards. Now good-time girls flag you down at noon from the dunes out Muizenberg way. Then you had to go out to the airport to see the poor in their cartoon shanties. Now you find tents under downtown flyovers, shacks on the slopes above Hout Bay. And now you hear gunshots at night.

Mandela did work his genie magic. For a time you had euphoria and the high-fiving, folk mixing it up and jiving. And all money is no longer in white hands. And there's no roof on how far you can go. No law to hobble you if you are born black or coloured. Yet, despite his magic, the ghosts of the past just won't fade out. And for a lot of shanty-town folk *freedom* is just a word, as hazy as *irony*. For such folk zilch has changed. Other than the colour of their *chief.* That's what's so ironic.

The place is stark and wind-scoured. Just a scattering of houses by the slipway. A few joints licensed to cage-dive. A bar or two, like a set in a cowboy film. The Freelander's parked in front of a makeshift warehouse. Wind whistles off the sea. Gulls see-saw on the keels of upturned boats. Otherwise lifeless. Not a dog in sight.

Inside the ill-lit joint they got a bar and a bicycle shop and a blonde flicking through a magazine. Bicycle frames hang like skeletons from dangling wires. A beautiful Breezer catches my eye. On a flat TV over the bar: a video of slick, silvery sharks gliding languidly by. I imagine the video was shot from a cage. It's as if I am looking into a fish tank with the great whites reduced to the scale of reef sharks.

An old black guy's spinning the wheel of an upended bicycle to fine-tune the spokes till the wheel runs true. He's singing a Xhosa song riddled with recurring *clicks* and *pops*, his tongue clicking in the hollow of his cheeks as if he's cajoling a lazy donkey.

The girl licks a fingertip now and then, before flicking over another page. Her eyes hover on a photo of a naked ginger-haired girl riding a white horse along a beach.

– You like her? she says without glancing up at me.

I want to say: I like just one girl. I like every fish-belly-pale inch of her. I love her wings and her way of luring birds. And if I can't have her I'll pine for her forever.

– She's pretty, I say.

– Here. You can have her.

She tears the pic out of the magazine and hands it to me, then goes on flicking through static worlds. I fold it up and put it in my pocket.

– You never saw girls naked in the old SA, hey?

For me as a boy in Amsterdam this was old hat. One time my mother found a girly magazine in my desk drawer. Instead of scolding me she took a pen and drew an eyepatch over a girl's left eye and put it back. She could have drawn stars over her nipples but she inked out an eye instead. I knew it was her because she had a photo of that Jew warrior Dayan and his trademark eyepatch that she'd torn out of a newspaper years before. Dayan was a hero to her just as Bono was to me. It puzzled me, what she'd done. And yet I was too ashamed to ever ask why. Years later at school in Cape Town a hockey ball split the skin along my cheekbone. I drew a line with a red *Koki* on the face of one of her gnomes to mimic my wound. Perhaps by then, with my sister dead, she was too far gone to see what a random red line had to do with an eyepatch.

I just nod. Zero told me so. Not white girls. Just *potent* (his word), beaded Zulu tits on postcards from Durban.

– You want to go down? she says without looking up from her magazine.

I imagine she has cage-diving in mind.

– I'm scared.

She laughs and now checks me out from foot to head, eyes lingering midway.

– You're in the cage. They can't bite you. And if they did the men got guns.

Cool. And no doubt they'd be happy to shoot a random, cocky coloured out to *sabo* their gig.

– I'm glad you told me that.

– *Ja.*

She hands me a flyer full of shots of gaping-jawed sharks. Their eyes are glazed with that distant, ashamed look dogs get when you catch them peeing.

– That's a lot of money. Is it cheaper for locals?

– How local?

I'm on the verge of telling her Hermanus but am keen to keep gun-toting men off my ass.

– Cape Town.

– Maybe I can let you go for this.

She pencils a figure on paper.

– That's still I lot. I'm a student.

I fiddle out my UCT student card from among the notes earned from hawking geckos. Still valid till the end of 2004.

– It's not cheap but you'd never forget it, hey? And in case you did, we shoot a video.

– You going out again today?

– We go out just once a day. Unless the sea's too wild.

– And you always see sharks?

– *Ja.* But if you don't, you can catch a free ride the day after.

– Aha.

– Sting did it.

– He went out on your boat?

– No. Another boat. But I saw him.

For a moment she looks downcast. Perhaps at the thought she had not hooked a film star and might forever be stranded in this end-of-the-line place.

– And if Sting goes out to sea you just got to pull a shark out of the hat, hey?

I nod. If ever there was a given, this is it.

– Catch is, sharks get lazy being chucked sardine chum all the time. It's like they're dazed.

– But don't they hunt seals for blubber?

– *Ja*. But something funny's happening. They look bored. Like lions in a circus, maybe. And tourists want to see them crazy for the chum.

– So how do you remedy that? Not go out as often?

– You change the chum. You see, it's not just the smell of blood the shark goes for, it's the signals from all the flapping.

– Flapping? You using live bait?

She leans over the counter, offering a tantalising view of yet another kind of bait.

– Don't tell anyone. But we just came up with a foolproof chum. It makes the sharks all perky.

I imagine she makes tourists rather perky as they order from the bar.

So this is the macabre fate of caught stray dogs. I wonder how they chuck them to the sharks so tourists don't see. Maybe Zodiac out to sea beforehand?

Now she goes all stiff and formal.

– So, mister, you keen?

– I'll think about it.

– You do that. But you must be here by six if you want to go out. We have to teach you a few things about cage-diving. Not that there's a risk. But just in case, hey?

I order an aptly named Honey Blonde Ale from her. As she bends to fetch it out of an icebox, a sparrow flies into the bar and weaves through the hanging bicycle frames.

I recall one time at school in Cape Town when a bird got trapped in the canteen. It flapped against the glass out of fear of the ungodly din. Boys tossed things at it. I took off my school shirt and flung it over the bird to catch it. I felt the sting of peach pips and bottle tops and pencils on my skin as I took the bird out. I felt shivers of the bird's fear through the cloth. I got a kind of revenge a few days afterwards by blowing into an empty soda bottle to mimic the tone of the school bell. Like dogs in an experiment, all boys within hearing radius stood up and without glancing at the clock headed out. Others followed till the canteen was empty. They discovered they'd been tricked when they got to class and found no teacher in sight.

The beer froths up as she jams a sliver of lemon into the mouth of the bottle, Mexican style. She catches the overflow with her tongue.

– Sorry, hey.

I just smile a half smile.

The sparrow flies out into the glare of the backyard. I follow it, squinting into the white light. At the end of the yard is a wavy zinc wall painted pink with a few sickly palms dangling yellow fans over it. I can't see over the wall.

I jump out of my skin as a baboon hisses at me from one end of the yard.

Beer froths out of the bottle again and the girl laughs before she goes back to flipping through her magazine.

Now I see he's on a wire running up to a kind of washing line that lets him shuttle back and forth. The grass under the line is worn to dust. His ass is an obscene shark-gum pink.

– Good baboon, I tell him.

He goes berserk, tugging on his wire and flashing his fangs. Hard to tell if he's flirting or in ninja mode.

The girl glances up and flicks me a smile. I lift the beer bottle as if to say cheers before thumbing the lemon down into the beer. It floats like some frilly, yellow-spined foetus in the liquid. I swig the beer: lemon and malt. A hint of honey in the smell.

Then I see a half-flat football on the grass. I put the beer down in the grass and juggle the dud ball from foot to foot. It's tricky, as there's no life in it.

The baboon hops up and down, reels off a volley of barks.

I flick the ball over the zinc.

I skirt round the baboon and jump to catch the rim of the zinc wall. I toe up and peer over. I see a row of cages. Just one of them has a dog in it. Deaf dog didn't hear the baboon barking or my feet clanging against the zinc. No sign of that mussel-licking Rhodesian dog.

I can't hold on long as the zinc rim cuts into my palms. I am about to let go when I hear the girl yell and before I can spin my head I'm yanked off the zinc. I fall hard to the grass.

The guy who tugged me down looms over me, burly as a rugby hooker.

– What the hell you after?

Winded, I gasp for air and hold up a hand for mercy.

– You spying on us, hey?

– No. No. I'm sorry. I just kicked a football over.

– Forget the ball and piss off, you hear.

– But I haven't finished my beer.

The guy kicks the bottle. It cracks against the pink zinc.

The old Xhosa man somehow slides through a gap in the zinc. I hear a listless bark. The ball flies over to us.

The hooker picks it up and cuts a slit in it with one swing of his pocketknife. The ball farts a gasp of sour air. You don't need a master's degree to decipher the symbolism.

40

Table mountain, Cape Town.

Under the pines at Kloof Nek, Zero lets the farmer out of the boot. He bolts, but Canada Dry dives him down.

Now Zero holds his Colt to his head.

– You walk along the jeep track ahead of us. If you sidestep, I shoot you.

The white stones of the track glow in the moonlight.

The smell of pines floats on the cool air.

The farmer walks ahead up along the looping track, spitting out gobbledygook. Perhaps a prayer, or a curse.

Zero hobbles after him, followed by Canada Dry. Whenever the farmer falters, Zero spurs the barrel of his Colt into his spine.

He must wonder, Zero thinks, *how you can be guffawing with your mates one moment, slinging down sherry, your cock jutting at the girl*

*you ripped bare . . . and then be reduced to a stooped, jibbering thing
the next.*

They are too high to hear the sounds of the shipyards and Canada Dry cuts his chirps. Apart from the farmer's blurred words and
the *chocking* of boots the night is silent.

Zero had thought of letting Phoenix toss him into the sea in
Shark Alley. He remembers the rush of cold fear he had felt when
the shark hit him and the unbearable lacuna as it looped before taking a half-moon out of him. Condemning him to hobble for life.
And to long flannels down to his snakeskins.

*But Jerusalem would freak out. Even if you told him this bastard
raped girls and this was his just comeuppance, Jero would go all John
Lennon on you. Ironic that he, a would-be poet, is blind to the beauty
of poetic justice. Yet it's not just about hiding gore from Jerusalem. If the
sharks jawed this fucker dead they'd never find a hint of him again. He'd
be gone one time, like that old lady a great white took in Fish Hoek just
the other day. In that case folk saw it happen, so there was no need to
find a corpse to put it on the front page of all the papers.*

In this case, as in all his other vigilante acts to date, they'll need
to find a cadaver if Zero is to get his curiously warped thrill from
reading about it in the paper.

He recalls the headlines so far:

CORPSE OF RED MAFIA MAN FOUND DOWN OLD
TIN MINE

That man would never again put a Jiffy over the head of a go-go
girl.

And just yesterday: ASIAN MAN FALLS TO HIS DEATH IN
SEA POINT

It is indeed a time for falling, reflects Zero.

– I need to piss, Canada Dry whines.

– Halt, Zero commands the farmer.

Out of years of reservist habit the farmer halts in two steps. *You can't take the army out of the Boer*, thinks Zero. *You always see on the newsreels that right-wing farmer riding his horse and his cult following of diehard Boers saluting their swastika-type flag and calling for a white republic. His name's White Earth. No joke. He just got out of jail for beating a petrol jockey half dead. He spends a few years in jail and the jockey's fucked up for life. That's justice for you. And old White Earth is a poet to boot. He comes out of jail mouthing pussy lines about dancing daffodils.*

– Funny they never need to piss in cowboy flicks, hey?

Canada Dry *tee-hees* at Zero's wit.

Below them the lights of Cape Town flicker like a zillion fireflies. You can see strings of fairy lights on cargo ships moored in the bay. You can see out to the dark arc of False Bay down to the left, and out over the Cape Flats to the jagged black spine of the Hottentots Holland range on the horizon.

They come to the Woodhead Reservoir. From here there's a long drop down to a ravine. Zero spits into the void. It would do the trick but there's a chance he'd snag on the way down. That would slow his fall and he might just survive.

The farmer falls silent, sensing his words are wasted.

They go on and now the track becomes a path cutting through thick *fynbos* and over boulders. The farmer falters, gasping for air.

The moon films the *fynbos* in quicksilver. Zero picks a feather of *fynbos* and rubs it between his fingers for the lemony scent. *How beautiful it is*, thinks Zero. *Like being on another planet. It begs you to come up with a poem.*

They go on till the world falls away below them to the lights of Camps Bay and the slopes of the Twelve Apostles beyond. You can just see the white hem of the sea. A flat rock juts out over the void. It defies the laws of physics, this rock. Like the Finger of

God. The drop's twice as long as from the reservoir. And no risk of snagging.

– You stand on that rock.

Zero recalls the time they picnicked on this rock. He and Miriam, before Jero was born and before they went into exile. They'd filled their mouths with champagne and French-kissed while it fizzed on their tongues. The champagne had gone to his head and he'd danced a risky jig on the edge till Miriam had peeled her shirt off to lure him to her. They'd felt the heat of the day's sun seep up from the rock into their naked skin, as if by osmosis. They'd felt as if their love would last forever. Zero laughs a short, dry laugh. *Perhaps Jero began his life on this very rock. Now how's that for poetry?*

– Now you jump.

The farmer's face is chalky white against the slate sky.

– All this flying reminds me of apartheid, Canada Dry remarks. Folk falling out of high windows, falling down stairwells, falling from a scaffold . . . falling, falling, falling.

He laughs a wry laugh for times gone by. Perhaps he feels a wistful pang for a time when it was clear who was being fucked over by whom.

– I beg you guys. You can have my Cherokee. You can have my farm. And all my sheep. Hey?

– And how do you want to heal the girls you raped?

– It was a sin, man. I was mad. I had scorpions in my skull.

– Scorpions? You telling me it wasn't your fault? You sound like that Greek madman whose tapeworm told him to stab Verwoerd. Thing is, he was a hero in my eyes for killing a racist bastard. You, on the other hand, are one sorry specimen.

– It was a sin. I prayed to Jesus in your car boot. And he pardoned me. It was as if I came out that boot reborn.

– Booted up from scratch, Canada Dry quips.

– Unlucky for you I don't hang out with Jesus. And if I did, I'd tell him how uncool I find it of him to let you off the hook. It was a sin. And now you suffer for it. Not for long. Not as long as the girls have to carry images of you in their head. So, you see, in that sense you are lucky. Now jump, man. Otherwise I shoot you in the gut . . . and you fall anyway.

– You're fucking crazy.

– Amen.

The farmer casts his eyes out over the Atlantic. Dawn lends the sea a gunmetal patina. Perhaps he thinks it ironic for a farmer who has spent a lifetime with his feet firm on the earth to die in the sky by the sea. Shadows shift like rippling black cloth over the Twelve Apostles: grimly silent jurors all. He finds no hint of mercy.

He teeters on the rim of the rock till Canada Dry's foot sends him over.

41

Hermanus. Dawn.
   Phoenix revs up a Cherokee with a Zodiac in tow. And Dove Bait riding shotgun.

I hop into the seat behind.

You can tell by the way he swings the wheel with one flat palm that the sass of Bahaya the taximan still lurks in his blood.

– Hey Phoenix. Hey Dove Bait. Cool you found a rubber duck.

– Borrowed from the Hawston boys.

A typical, laconic Phoenix one-liner. You'd think Clint Eastwood rather than Freud was his mentor.

– And the jeep?

– That's a longer story.

Dove Bait caws as if this is a good joke.

Phoenix swivels his head to scowl at him. At that moment something goes *pop* under a tyre. Phoenix squints into the rearview.

– You asshole! You made me kill a tortoise.

I have never seen Phoenix rattled before. When he ran down old Black Mamba, it was in cold blood. He is forever cool and lucid.

– All the years I rode a taxi I never ran down a dog.

– Sorry, tunes Dove Bait.

Fortunately Dove Bait senses it's not the time to remind him of Black Mamba.

– But a tortoise can't feel like a dog.

– You ever got into the head of a tortoise, hey? He's not a fucking flower. He feels pain. He falls in love. Maybe he dreams. Who can tell all he can remember? Or if he can foresee his own death?

Dove Bait just gapes out at the world. This topic has got too loaded for him.

– Poor tiddly tortoise, tuts Phoenix.

Somehow Phoenix's hard, bald head reminds me of a tortoise shell and I feel faint after the sound of that shell imploding. I wind down the window for air.

There's a pepperminty smell to the blur of *fynbos*. I hear the defiant call of a bird from the lagoon. I think of boys dozing in a London bus. I feel a yearning for my mother's coffee and her way of haunting that limbo between dream and waking.

– That boy going to man your stall again?

– He is. He's keen to earn money for medicine for his mother. AIDS is killing her.

I picture Buyu lugging a box the size of an Indian tea box from my flat to the market. Then I picture Buyu's father staring at the sun peeling off the surface of Lake Victoria and of his mother lying in the lee of a dhow, pining for a distant son.

– Hey Phoenix, you told my old man about the priest's dog?

– Did. But he had something to get rid of. Sent *him* along for the ride instead.

He disdainfully flicks his head at Dove Bait, who has gone all mute and meek.

I hear Zero's voice in my head: *I leave no spoor. No proof.*

– How we going to follow them out to sea without spooking them? There's no way they'll chuck a dog to the sharks in front of us.

– I got a plan. We don't follow them. We go out to Shark Alley before they do. We hover behind Geyser Rock in this Zodiac and hope they swing in. Tourists want to see seals *and* sharks. A double bill. They hope to see a shark kill a seal. But the sharks will zero in on the dog instead if he's bleeding. I'm hoping they'll spill fish blood rather than cut him.

– That's the plan? To hide behind a rock until they drop him overboard . . . and just hope they don't cut him up beforehand?

– And we let him doggy-paddle till we catch a fin on film.

– But that's a fucked-up plan. He's old, that dog. He'll sink. Or the sharks'll kill him before we can fish him out.

– A dog in water's a demon. He's not just going to go down like some Chinaman caught in a rip tide.

– Can't we just fetch him out of his cage now? Go in with guns blazing and . . .

– We have to catch them red-handed . . . otherwise this will just go on. I want to film it.

– But I *know* this dog.

– You told me he's old and deaf. Maybe it'd be a mercy. On the other hand, he may just get lucky. Depends on how we time it. I want to shut down this gig today. I got another job up north to handle. Me, Zero, Canada Dry, this palooka lover-boy here . . . and that Zimbo I told you of. We'll be gone over Christmas. Hope you'll be cool.

– Christmas was never a focus for us.

– Still. Call your old lady up. Somehow she's less dazed. It's as if this Zimbo has cast some kind of voodoo to lure her out of her sorrow.

I wonder if his voodoo can cure her. I would kill to see my mother laugh again the way she did that time when Zero's foot went through the floor in Amsterdam. She'll smile in that distant, dreamy way of hers when she's hanging out with her gnomes, but she no longer laughs.

And I wonder about this yellow lab. I wonder why they sacrificed that young harbour dog, the Rhodesian, and left this dud old dog on death row. Perhaps that dog was friskier bait and they had to lure a shark for Leonardo DiCaprio. Maybe they fear sharks would spit him out as he's all hide and sinew. Or perhaps the priest can work some kind of voodoo too. I hope his prayers keep the lab afloat in a fourteen-degree sea so cold it knifes to the bone.

Rub-a-dub-dub, three men in a tub. And who do you think they be? The *zen*-darter, the floozy-killer and me, all floating in a Zodiac.

Curious seals glide under the Zodiac or bark at us from their island.

Through binoculars I see their Zodiac come into focus. Two men and the dog. The dog puts his head into the wind and his ears flap flippantly as if he's just going for a ride. He can't bite at the wind as dogs do, for they have bound a bandana around his snout to muzzle him.

They cut the motor. I fear they'll see us peering over rocks painted white by seagull guano, but they are too focused on fiddling with the dog. They tie a ball of sardine chum to a float and then tie the float to the end of his tail. They undo the bandana just as they sling him overboard. The dog goes under, then bobs up: chin jutting out, front feet all a-frenzy, eyes glassy with fear. He paws at the Zodiac but they jab at him with an oar as if dipping a sheep. Each jab draws a yelp before he goes under. Each time I hold my breath until his head buoys up again.

Now he doggy-paddles in circles, his feet sending telltale volts through the sea. He trolls the bobbing chum from his tail, and the chum unspools a thread of blood that a shark can smell a quarter of a mile away.

– Lucky they didn't cut him, chirps Dove Bait.

Somehow *lucky* is hardly the word to describe a dog about to be gobbled up by a shark.

Again the dog swims for the Zodiac. They listlessly row away from him, hands shading their eyes from the low sun.

Phoenix is panning his camera to and fro.

Now I see him through my binoculars: his fin slitting seamlessly through the blue.

– *Shaaark!* I cry.

Phoenix focuses his lens.

The sea's so limpid you can see his outline: a long, lucid, silver-skinned torpedo.

I shiver in horror.

– Let's go, I beg.

– Not yet.

He has to catch fin and dog in the same frame.

– Forget proof. This is crazy!

Another few toe-pinching seconds go by.

Now Phoenix signals a thumbs up and Dove Bait fires up the Yamaha. We gun in from due east, the bow of the Zodiac jousting high over the sea. The shark's due west.

The guys on the other Zodiac head out, spooked by this unforeseen twist. In the distance we see the tourist speedboat on the horizon. Today the Great White, tomorrow the Big Five. Or a tour of Soweto.

We converge from polar points. The distance between dog and shark is now maybe a javelin throw. This shark's a demon. He does not circle as they do in films. He zeroes in on the chum and the furry of the flapping-footed dog. Phoenix judges we won't get to the dog in time. He fires a shot at the fin, hardly the measure of a matchbox from this angle.

The guys in the fleeing Zodiac duck as the shot rings out.

The bullet's nicked a chink out of his fin, yet the shark's unfazed. Its conical head shoots out of the water. His jaws flash a riot of jagged, jumbled teeth. He snatches the chum and shakes his head, flicking the dog to and fro as frivolously as a high sea plays with a surfboard on a leash. Another shot puts a hole through the fin. Now the shark keels to flash his white belly at the sky. Now he dives, yanking the dog down after him.

We fly over the blood-tinted wake of the chum. I see the shark spearing down deep under us. Phoenix fires yet another shot.

Dove Bait spins the Zodiac on the blood-tinted surface.

Phoenix's bald head looks sallow as a ghoul. He pockets his gun.

– He was a good nineteen foot, Dove Bait tunes. A fucking Zeppelin!

The float surfaces.

I dig the heels of my hands into my eyes. I feel Phoenix mussing my hair. Then I hear Dove Bait whoop.

The dog's come up! His tail's bleeding an absurdly vivid magenta. The shark's teeth cut it down to a stump. I gaff him by his collar and yank him on board. He stands on shaky feet, then shudders the sea from his sorry hide. I go down on my knees to hug him: deaf, docked, old dog. He sneezes in my face and wags his raw stump.

There's no sign of the tourist boat or the Zodiac.

In the distance, another shark hits a rogue seal. He shoots all the way out of the sea. In the sky he twists his head to gulp the squalling seal.

I recall fishing from the harbour wall in Kalk Bay at sundown with old Zero. It was 1994. I was fourteen. We'd been in the Cape again for two years. The mood was festive. Mandela was out. Hope was kiting high. I hand-lined into the harbour and Zero cast a line out to sea. The fish I'd hooked floated among beers in the cooler box. Zero was shooting the breeze with the other coloured fisherman. Then my line sung out. The gut cut into my palm. I let go and sucked at my hand. The shark surfaced, flipped, and then he was gone. I yelled *Shaaark* at all the fisherman gazing out to sea. They dropped their rods to come and stare into the flat, oily green water. I measured it out in footsteps to prove it to them. Eleven feet. Heel to toe. They shook their heads and giggled toothlessly as they drifted away. Zero mussed my hair and said it was a seal that took my line. Or it got hooked in the propeller of that trawler just heading out into open sea. Afterwards my mother and sister joined us for lemon tart at the Olympia Café. My mother winked at me as if to say *my wistful dreamer, my floating poet.* I so wished I'd had it on film. Just the rubbing of the sole of my sister's foot against the arc of mine saved me from crying at the injustice of it. I smiled at her and that was the last time I can recall looking into her eyes.

Now I see another two fins gliding towards us. The clan has arrived.

I remember Zero telling us then in that café the story of a shark landing in a boat called *Lucky Jim* and his flipping one of the crew into the sea.

Suddenly the Zodiac feels far too flimsy under us.

42

A farm an hour out of Cape Town. Afternoon.

Phoenix and Jabulani look down from the slopes of the Simonsberg on the mosaic of vineyards and dams below. This is the valley Cecil John Rhodes called his. He spent money he made from diamonds dug out of the hole in Kimberley on Dutch farms until all you see below you was in his hands. From here he would gaze out over Africa and remember the dry stone towers of a medieval city far to the north called Great Zimbabwe. He'd think of the birds carved out of stone that he filched from the ruins and wonder at the mystery of how empires always fall. It would have been hard for him, then, to imagine the fall of yet another empire so vast the sun never set on it . . . the empire he was a lord of.

Jabulani thinks of how he spent his youth in a country called

Rhodesia, named after this same Rhodes. And how some of the whites who ruled it then had scorned the theory that Great Zimbabwe was the handiwork of native Zimbabweans. So deep did their racism go. He recalls a journey to the ruins and squinting through the glare of the sun to make out in a boulder the form of the Zimbabwean bird. This was (he had told Panganai and Tendai) the distant land of Ophir that Solomon got his cargo gold from. This was the El Dorado of Africa. He'd had a way then of spinning out a yarn: *And not just gold . . . but ivory and gems and monkeys and peacocks. So great was Zimbabwe.* And now his country had become the joke of the world.

And Ophir was perhaps never in Africa after all, but in India or beyond.

Phoenix puts up a row of empty beer cans on the banks of the Good Hope dam.

He measures out a distance along the dam wall akin to the gap between wickets in cricket. He hands Jabulani a .38 revolver.

– I told you, I am not a cowboy. I am a teacher.

– This is not about splitting infinitives, teacherman. If your bullet doesn't split this Ghost Cowboy's skull one time, you are smoked. *Capito?* History.

Jabulani squints at the beer cans. They warp in the mirage shimmering up from the sand. The gun feels cool against his scar. He fires. Sand spurts up between the cans. He glances timidly at Phoenix.

But Phoenix just stares at the cans.

Jabulani fires another shot. This time a can tilts as dirt flicks up. Yet the can doesn't fall.

Phoenix nods.

– That girl at the Shell. Focus on her.

Jabulani sees Ghost Cowboy's shotgun twirl her so flippantly.

The film in his head spools out at just a few frames per second. He sees how her bare feet dance a spinning tarantella. He sees the blood seep through her shirt like a blooming of red flowers. Her one hand flings out so flamboyantly you'd be forgiven for thinking Ghost Cowboy just let her go at the end of a tango. That he'll maybe catch her flying hand and pluck her towards him again. The other hand goes to her gut as if to pick her red flowers.

This time a can skips into the sky. Then another. And Phoenix is smiling.

– So you can teach an old dog new tricks. You have a good eye. All you needed was to focus.

Jabulani smiles like a schoolboy who scored well on a paper.

Phoenix picks a peach and skins it in one skilled spiral.

– This is the valley where I spent my boyhood. My pa picked this kind of peach. Yellow cling, they call it. So sugar-sweet and sappy, man.

His lips slit into a rueful smile.

– I thought this was a *Cape* thing: this peach. As Cape as Cape gooseberry and *hanepoot*. Now books tell me peaches come all the way from China and gooseberry's South American as tango. And that the Egyptians made wine from this same *hanepoot* grape. Fucking Cleopatra had *hanepoot*. I tell you, everything you'd put your head on the block for as hard-core fact, every benchmark you think is fixed, turns out to be an illusion. Take light. You'd think it's just waves, hey?

Jabulani nods.

– Whereas, in fact . . .

Phoenix lets this thought drift out of focus.

– One *fact* I was taught as a schoolboy on this farm was that all the beautiful things in this world belonged to the white man: the peaches, the wine, the gold, the diamonds, the beaches. And even as a boy I thought: No. My pa planted the trees, my pa slaves on this farm under a bastard sun. I'll pick the fruit if I want to. And then one day the white farmer zoomed up in his Isuzu pickup. I had no hope of outrunning his pickup, so I flung the yellow clings away. I hoped he'd just zoom by, but he halted. He found the peaches in the sand. They might have been windfall peaches if not for telltale tooth marks.

Phoenix laughs a curbed, bitter laugh at his folly.

He yelled at me to jump onto his pickup. I howled and begged but he felt no pity. I saw his son in the front of the pickup. A boy who went to a fancy school for white boys in town where they had an athletics track and a swimming pool. A boy heading for university. A boy who had his fruit cut and peeled for him by a coloured maid.

Phoenix spits out the pip of his peach.

– The police took me into the courtyard and gave me a hiding with a cane and then let me go. Two cuts. That was it. They said they had no time to go to court with me. They said I was lucky I'd got off lightly. The thing that stung for years was not the caning . . . but that the white boy, a boy just like me who dreamed girls and blew Chappies bubbles and played football barefoot, did not glance at me on that trip to the police station. He held his stare ahead. All the way I thought: If he just looks into my eyes, just once, he'll see himself in me and beg his father to let me go.

Phoenix shakes his head and whistles through his teeth.

– My father was gutted. After all the years of picking peaches, he felt he could never look the farmer in his eyes again. It was beyond him to doubt the white man's wisdom. He said I had dirtied his name. Not long afterwards I dropped out of school and went to Cape Town. I hid in the hulls of boats in the dry docks and dreamed of sweet, forbidden peaches while hunger taunted me.

— But how'd you get a foot in the door?

— I did things. Cruel things. Crazy things.

There's a long, laden lull punctuated by the electric clicks of grasshoppers.

— Hey Phoenix, how come Zero risks his life again and again to fight this war of his?

— It was the year of freedom and Zero was on a high. I was not in the picture then, but this is how the story goes. His daughter took the train to Muizenberg to go swim in the sea. Miriam was always wary of her travelling alone but Zero laughed at her fears. Some-where between Muizenberg station and the sea, maybe somewhere along the Zandvlei lagoon, a man jumped her. They found her in the dunes beyond Khayelitsha. She was bare. She had scratches on her face that looked like the claw marks of a leopard. And her hands were marred.

Jabulani pictures Tendai so innocently hula-hooping in a world riddled with evils she can't yet imagine.

— The police did not find the killer. Years later, this was while I was hiding in Zero's attic, there was a report in the paper about a young girl killed in Langa. Again they found leopard marks on her. There was a lot in the papers about the Leopard Killer striking again. Some folk thought that he literally morphed into a leopard at night. This time he was sloppy and did not see the old tramp lying zonked out in the shadows on cheap *shebeen* beer. He was too shit scared to come forward, this old tramp, fearing the po-lice would put the blame on him. But I found him, and a bottle of White Horse was all it took to get the low-down on the killer: his lagging left foot, the moonlit diamond in his tooth. It took half a year to track him down. In all this time the police had no luck. Maybe they saw it as just another murder docket in this land plagued by murder.

Jabulani looks down on the vineyards and china-blue dams below and thinks: *How ironic that a land so beautiful can be so bloodthirsty.*

– But let me tell you, Jabulani, I have never seen a man beg like he did to be put out of his pain.

He puts his hand into a pocket and pulls out a bit of paper. He gingerly unfolds it. Then Jabulani sees the sun glint in a diamond pinched between his fingertips.

43

Christmas Eve, 2004. Hermanus new harbour. After dusk.
Lotte comes in to Quayside Cabin with Al Pike and Zippo Dude.

My heart pummels against my ribs.

Al shoots a smile my way. To the other guys I am just a live jukebox.

Lotte's eyes flicker over me (the soles of my feet tingle), then she turns her gaze to the harbour where Buyu is hand-lining with the bus boys in the paling light (my feet go dead).

I play fervidly for her and yet she never tunes in. Her eyes shift from one to another without ever falling on me. At the end of a song her fingers flutter flippantly over her palm.

The skin of her thigh ripples like seersucker where it catches on the bench and her white dress rides high. She loves me.

She winds a rogue thread from the hem of her dress round a finger and snaps it. She loves me not.

She tips a pinch of salt onto the foot of the glass and dabs at it with a licked fingertip. She loves me.

She holds a cool wine glass to her forehead. She loves me not.

She sucks a mussel out of its black shell. She stabs at a whitebait with her fork and pops it, head, gut and fin, into her mouth. She loves me.

She studies the tacky flotsam hanging from the roof, her eyes lingering on a red Dali crayfish. She loves me not.

I envy that damn crayfish that catches her eye.

I play Coldplay blind. In my mind's eye I see the lazy sway of her hips before me, a Savanna bottle dangling from her fingers. Folk go on swigging beer and chattering. I alone see her concertina her dress in her free hand until it reveals her unfussy cowrie cleft. I alone see the fabric draw up higher still to free her nipples, sushi-salmon pink. I alone see her slide a sliver of lime subtly over her shell and shiver at the sting of it.

And then the song's over and she's thumbing a lime down into her Savanna.

Out on the dark harbour Buyu and the others have abandoned their fishing to play a game with bottle tops. I see a tourist taking photos of the boys. A cormorant dives from the mast of a fishing boat and surfaces with a fish sparking silver in the flashlight of a camera.

I wish I was free to just dive for the thing I yearn for.

A waiter puts a cold beer down on my amp.

– Cheers, I say.

– Sent over by the man in the far corner.

I lift the bottle of Windhoek and look into Al's eyes. He nods. A hint of a sly smile lurks in his lips. The way he holds my gaze,

I'd swear he feels it in his bones: that I have fucked his girl. Perhaps he pities me for being so madly hooked, for he does not kiss her in front of me like a dog marking out his hood. I wish he was an asshole, so I'd feel no guilt as he and I enact a mock clinking of glass against glass in the air and then each swig a gulp in sync.

Lotte's cheeks hollow as she sucks a cocktail of ice cream and Kahlúa through a straw.

Zippo Dude lights a glass of sambuca and swigs it down as it flames.

Al foots the bill.

As they go I see her scribble something on a coaster with the bill biro.

I abandon my playing midflow to save the coaster before a waiter can whisk it away.

I gaze over the wall into her yard. I see static shadow figures behind the curtains. I see her form drifting to and fro. Then she's on the veranda, sliding her feet into sandals, fluttering over the grass.

– A film. *Pulp Fiction*. Al's a Tarantino aficionado. They're killing a bottle of Jack Daniel's. I've maybe a quarter of an hour before Al figures out I'm gone.

I follow her down a rogue path to rocks by the sea.

– Surfers cut through and jump from the rocks at high tide.

Waves fling their moon-lust at the rocks. Junk (beer bottles, Bic lighters, shotgun hulls, Red Bull shots, a jilted flip-flop, a tangle of fishing gut) is caught in the rock cracks.

She yanks down my Bermudas, bids me lie down on a flat rock. She ties my hands over my head with the fishing gut. I feel the balmy breath from her mouth on my lips. I feel the rock scratch my spine and the gut cut into my skin. She unzips me and I am in her mouth and I'm floating . . . until I see a rat just a yard from my left foot. I am in a catch-22. I sense I'm just a few notches away from nirvanic abandon and that the slightest shift in vibe will put her dream tempo out of kilter. All I need to do is stay cool and focused, shut out the rat's quivering whiskers and beady eyes. I pinch my toes against the inevitable jab of pain as its incisors punch into my skin. In the end raw fear overrides lust and she feels me go slack.

I see the quizzical slant of her brow as she spits me out.

– No good?

The rat's gone galley west and I wonder if she'll think I dreamed it.

– It was magic . . . but there was a rat. I'm sorry.

– That was to be your Christmas gift. From your white angel.

She tames her dress and combs her fingers through her hair.

– I love you, I tell her.

She just kisses me on the forehead. I shut my eyes to imbibe her scent. When I look again she's gone, leaving me to free my hands with my teeth.

I feel deserted, robbed, gutted. At the thought of him lying over her on white linen in a ratless space, I want to choke myself with the fishing line.

44

Christmas Day, 2004. N1 highway, heading north through the Karoo.

Jabulani rides shotgun beside old Zero in his mystic-green Benz through a land of yellow and ochre and olive tones. Behind them Canada Dry's shooting play-play shots at lone birds on telegraph poles.

Phoenix and Dove Bait follow in the Jeep Cherokee.

They go through lonely *dorps* each with their high church, butchery, dim hotel, glass-finned jail, take-away café. In the windows of shut shops they see tacky tinsel and fake snow. The streets are deserted. All the folk are in church in this good, god-fearing land.

Jabulani has a feeling of unreality. As if he's in a dream. Not too long ago he was in a school where there was a low risk of being killed. A boy might snap his collarbone in rugby or twist his foot in the long jump. A teacher might trip over a school bag left in the hallway or fall off his bicycle. None had ever died. This is kamikaze crazy: heading for a shoot-out with the devil. He wants to beg Zero to spin the Benz around . . . but if he does he'll be forever haunted by the caught Zimbabweans: zombie-eyed, stoop-spined, lost to the world. Jabulani imagines them imagining him in Cape Town: a mouth full of fish and wine, their hard lot on that death farm the furthest thing from his mind.

Jabulani calls up an image of Miriam alone with her gnomes and cat. Zero had found a waterfront bar that would hire the two Zimbabwean girls over Christmas and New Year. They just wanted pretty girls; otherwise Jabulani would have jumped at the job. He'd far rather carry beers over his head to tourists than tote a gun for handouts from Zero. Then again, if he's to be frank, *handouts* is perhaps too cynical a word for the good money he'd earned so far on jobs where he'd been just a fumbling, unneeded tagger-on.

Miriam. He finds her sallow skin and far-gazing eyes beautiful. He is puzzled by Zero's curt, offhand way with her. No doubt it has to do with the girl they lost. Perhaps Miriam had not let him into her sorrow then. And that had sapped their love dry. He flinches at the thought of Zero making love to her. Him, bulky as a rugby hooker, seesawing over the fulcrum of her fragile hips.

He has fallen in his own eyes. He's always thought of himself as a good father and a faithful lover, yet now he's curious – no, keen – to feel his dark skin yin-yang with hers, subtly opaque and silky, to hold her opaline tits in his palms.

As if reading his thoughts, Zero swings the Benz hard off the road, shooting up smoky dust.

They picnic on Kentucky and ice-cold Black Label beer under bluegums.

The sun burns down on the tar. A curious buzzard eyes them

from a telegraph pole. A few white woolly dots at the foot of a distant windmill. Otherwise no hint of life.

But now a hazy scarecrow figure drifts into focus. A bony old music-maker in a dusty top hat and a floppy suit plucking a tune from his guitar and singing along: a freewheeling, flirty yet lackadaisical tune riddled with recurring cow-cajoling whistles. He reconfigures time to his whim, this black Dylan, and so walks the long miles without the measure of distance sapping his vigour. He's so lost in his mesmeric groove that he would have gone by without blinking an eyelid had the dog on his heels not barked.

They all stare at this phantom, this relic of a vanishing Africa. Jabulani has heard of Zulu *maskandi* minstrels, just as he has heard of Indian holy men who can float in the air. Such a man is not just nomadic busker, but poet, prophet, storyteller and walking history book. But why on earth is he on a road so far from KwaZulu-Natal? The world is standing on its head.

Zero offers him a Kentucky drumstick and a tall boy of beer. Tells him: *Happy Christmas.*

The man tips his hat for this *Christmas box* and walks on. He hands the drumstick to the dog. Jabulani wonders if he survives on liquid alone, like an air plant or the myth of a Masai surviving on blood and milk. He walks on along the mustard dust between the jagged rim of the tar and the riot of cosmos.

Jabulani feels a sudden pang for the red dust of Zimbabwe and wonders if he will ever see her again.

45

Christmas Day, 2004. Hermanus. Before dawn.

Buyu and I pick cannas and hibiscus along the cliff path. We fill a wine box with the petals.

We scatter the petals on the grass on front of her house, then hide. The seagulls and sparrows call her out.

She wanders barefoot out over the mosaic of petals, yellow, orange and red. She flings bread to the gulls and sparrows and *dassies*.

Al comes out onto the veranda, a mug of smoking coffee in hand.

– Magic, hey? says Lotte.

– Looks like an Indian funeral, says Al.

Buyu and I ride the Vespa out past Fisherhaven to Kleinmond for Christmas lunch.

Flamingos fly like a school of pink fish through the blue of the sky.

The water level has sunk low in the Fisherhaven lagoon. Wild horses drift through a sea of red amphibian flowers.

How weird, to spend half the year underwater dreaming of the sun.

We picnic down on the Kleinmond slipway. I have takeaway tuna sushi with flamingo-pink ginger and a beer. Buyu (who laughs at my forking out good money for uncooked fish) has fish and chips and Sprite.

Seagulls hustle Buyu for the chips. They too scorn my sushi.

The sea is alluringly blue, yet kelp sways darkly below her skin.

One lone penguin weaves through the kelp.

Buyu wanders down to the water. He pinches a crab between my chopsticks and holds it up for me to see.

– Free sushi, he jokes.

I laugh, though in my gut I feel robbed of Lotte.

Buyu lets the crab go.

He skips crab-flat stones over the surface of the water. I imagine he's remembering a lakeshore in Tanzania. I wonder if his mother's hanging on.

And I think of my mother. How she, so adored by her tacky dwarves, may feel less lonely than me.

I shut my eyes against the falling sun. In the psychedelic red sea behind my eyelids, I see a kind of dancing, four-handed Kali: nude, fanged and red-eyed. Her skin changes colour, now blue, now black. In one hand she holds a gun, in another a *panga*, in another diamonds, in yet another gold. She has a string of skulls hanging from her head. The dusty skulls of Biko and other folk killed by apartheid. The shiny skulls of folk who thought freedom would kill all the old demons. And one skull of a girl whose fingers wizardly turned string into diamonds or a cat's eye or a star.

46

Boxing Day, 26 December 2004. Somewhere south of the Limpopo. Before sunrise.

For miles now they have been cruising. Jabulani's head juts out the wound-down window, his eyes peeled for the sun-bleached ox skull on a pole. He fears they may have gone too far. That it somehow eluded him. Perhaps it hangs at such an angle that it does not reflect light if you travel from the south. Nina had been heading south then. Or perhaps Ghost Cowboy got rid of the thing in the veld, for it was Jabulani's sole signpost to the farm. He curses himself for not having put down another marker . . . a pyramid of stones, or a snatch of cloth tied to the barbed wire.

He thinks of Nina and how cool and crazy she'd been. If he survives this, he'll go and see her in hospital.

On the horizon he sees a luminous hint of dawn. If the skull did not pop up out of the dark soon, they'd have to abandon their plan. It all hung on timing. Zulus always raided at dawn, Zero had said, to catch their foe out in that murky, eye-tricking time when it is no longer night and not yet day. And on this dawn of the day after Christmas, the gunmen would be doubly muddy-headed from boozing hard. That's what Zero's gambling on. For a few miles now there'd been a loaded stillness in the Benz. Zero had switched off the radio and Canada Dry had run out of jokes.

If he fails to find the skull, not only will he have put Zero and his crew out, but there was a good chance old Jonas would die on that damned farm.

And then the Benz's headlights illuminate the skull: sinister and grinning.

– Whoa! The skull! Jabulani cries.

– Cool, says Zero.

– *Bang, bang*, goes Canada Dry.

Jabulani is amazed Ghost Cowboy left the ox skull hanging. Perhaps he wanted to lure Jabulani to a showdown.

Zero blinks to signal to the Cherokee. They halt maybe half a mile beyond the skull. They kill the lights and go by foot along the tar and then along the dirt road to the farm. After a mile or so the road becomes an avenue through high, raggedy bluegums. At the end of the tunnel of trees is the farmhouse, ghostly in this looming dawn. To Jabulani this is a rerun of Bloemfontein.

Zero goes over the plan: Phoenix is to go ahead to *defuse the dogs* with his darts. Zero is to swing round to the east through the veld so he'll be silhouetted by the rising sun. Canada Dry and Dove Bait are to stay put on this road, hidden behind the bluegums, to cut off this escape route. Jabulani's job is to swing west through the veld and somehow warn the Zimbabweans trapped in the barn . . . before the bullets begin to fly.

Jabulani tiptoes gingerly through the veld, scared of cracking a stick or snagging on a tripwire. He hears a two-toned iambic grunt and halts dead in his tracks. Another porcupine? A warthog? Then he figures it was the choked-off bark of one of the Dobermann dogs. Then he hears a curt bark, followed by a yelp fading to a whine. The other dog down, darted. A deep voice – from the farmhouse? – tells the dogs to *voetsek*. Jabulani sucks in a draft of air, holds it.

Now he runs flat out over the bare veld behind the barn, his borrowed boots chocking against stones, chipping the hard husk off anthills.

As he runs, he recalls how a steenbok had somehow got into a tennis court at the school in Bulawayo and how the schoolboys had taunted it: gaping-eyed, bat-eared, jittery-footed and absurdly out of context. It was the most vulnerable thing he'd ever seen until now. He feels as if he's haring across a firing range. He steels himself for the bite of a bullet. But no bullet is shot and now he's up against the far wall of the barn, gasping for air.

– Hey, Jonas! he calls through the wood joints of the barn. Jonas!

– Yo! Jonas cries.

You can tell he thinks it's a ghost or a hobgoblin come for him.

– Happy Christmas, Jonas. This is Jabulani.

– Hey, teacher! You survived! You fetched the police?

– No police. Just a few men.

How is he to describe them? Layabout vigilantes? Laid-back desperados? Tarantino types?

Jabulani hears sighs of disillusionment from the captives.

– But they are hard-core heroes.

There's a rippling murmur of hope from the Zimbabweans.

– When you hear shots I want you to hack your way out this side of the barn. You still got that watermelon *panga*?

– I got it.

– Where will you go?

– I go home to my wife in Zimbabwe. I go home empty-handed but I am too old for this. I will bake bread again if there is any flour to be found.

– I will see you, Jonas.

Now the sun's surfacing and Jabulani will be lit up the moment he juts his head round the corner. He puts his gun in his pocket and inches along on all fours to peek around. A bullet whizzes just over his head. Jabulani plucks his head back into the shaded lee of the barn. His heart beats frenziedly. Now he hears a volley of bemused shouts from the farmhouse and the muted murmurs of the Zimbabweans in the barn.

What happened to Phoenix? He took out the dogs, but how can a gunman be free to take a potshot at him? Perhaps Phoenix hadn't seen him and the guy was zoned out on a deckchair by the pool or the tennis court until the dog barked.

He wonders if Zero has got to the farmhouse yet.

Now Jabulani hears another shot. He figures Phoenix got the sniper. And then follows another volley of shots. Perhaps one of the other gunmen has gone down. There's a fermata of surreal silence, before the world explodes with gunfire.

Now he hears the roar of a motor. The army troop truck. The sound of the motor fades slightly. Then he hears shots and the motor cutting out. That'd be Canada Dry and Dove Bait waylaying the truck.

He takes another look round the corner. No one shoots at him. As he edges along the wall of the barn he hears the staccato sound of Jonas's *panga* blade biting into the wood of the barn and the muddled voices of the Zimbabweans.

At the far end of the barn he looks out onto the farmyard. Phoenix is hiding behind a tipped wheelbarrow, drawing all the flak from the farmhouse. Two dogs and a fallen gunman lie bleeding in the dust. Another gunman is in the swimming pool, tinting the water red.

Jabulani draws his gun. He sees Zero walking along the roof of the farmhouse.

Ghost Cowboy comes out of the house, holding a knife to the throat of the young black girl Jabulani howled for. Ghost Cowboy has a handgun in his free hand. They head towards the zebra-striped Land Rover.

Shots from Ghost Cowboy's gun spark off the barrow.

They dance a weird, spinning waltz, Ghost Cowboy and the girl, over the yard. She's got this white Rolling Stones T-shirt on with the image of that long, red, lolling tongue. The knife cuts a gill slit in her skin and blood filters out till the outlines of the tongue blur.

Jabulani draws a bead on Ghost Cowboy but dares not fire.

The hinges of the Land Rover door whine a high note. Ghost Cowboy flashes a defiant smile at his foes. At that instant of fuck-you cockiness Jonas jumps out from behind him like some mad samurai Puck. He swings his *panga* down through the albino's head to his eyes. There's a hiatus of horror before blood flows profusely and the girl's cry skirls to the sky.

Then the girl falls and a gut shot from Zero or Phoenix fells the cowboy. He kneels in the dust, the *panga* blade jutting out from his forehead, blood masking his face. He lets the knife go, turns the gun on himself, but his hand quivers too violently and he just shoots off an ear.

He's still alive when half a dozen Zimbabweans who did not skedaddle into the veld converge on him. They snatch the gun out of his hand, draw the *panga* blade out of his head and toss him over the wire to the crocodiles. Somehow he finds his feet again. Bloodblinded, he capers haphazardly till he falls into the pond. No killing frenzy follows, no deadly, scaly torpedoes zoom in on him through the water. The crocodiles have learnt long ago that there's nowhere for their prey to go.

Jonas hovers over the girl, dabbing up the blood with a hanky, soothing her with motherly clickings of his tongue.

Canada Dry and Dove Bait rumble up in the troop truck in time to see a giant crocodile dawdle-hobble along the rim of the pond. To see it catch Ghost Cowboy's flapping forearm in its jaw, toss its head up and tug off the arm as you might pluck a drumstick from a chicken, or pull a Christmas cracker apart. Another flick of its head and the arm's gone.

– Far out, chirps Canada Dry.

Jabulani fires two shots into Ghost Cowboy to end his pain. Each of the shots jigs his torso to and fro in the shallows.

The Zimbabweans stand hat in hand. Despite all he did to them, they bow to a man who died so macabre a death without crying out.

Jabulani's eyes pan the farmyard. The carnage reminds him of the ending of Hamlet.

The girl revives.

Dove Bait stares longingly at her. You can tell he wishes to have her as a memento.

– Pity about the guy in the pool. It's a beautiful day for a swim, chirps Canada Dry.

– You and Dove Bait fish him out, Zero commands. Chuck all the corpses over the wire to the crocs.

– And the dogs?

– Shoot them, Canada. Then they too go over.

– But . . . but they're *innocent.*

– How so?

– They're just dogs.

– You have a gift, jokes Zero. If I'm ever in the dock I'll call you to get me off the hook. Fact is, they'll starve otherwise. This way they won't feel a thing.

– Not my old dog, begs Jonas. Let him go with me to Zimbabwe.

– Just the darted dogs, says Zero.

The Zimbabweans don their hats again.

– Phoenix. Get these Zimbos to give you a hand loading this truck to the hilt with marijuana.

– That's a lot of dope, chirps Canada Dry.

– Leave space behind the cab for whoever wants to catch a ride down to Cape Town.

And to Jonas:

– You get to ride in that funky, zebra Land Rover. You and your dog. Just ditch it before the border.

– Daughter, you come home with me, Jonas says to the girl.

Dove Bait looks gutted.

Jabulani, aside, to Zero:

– You want to ferry a cargo of dope down the highway?

– I feel lucky, tunes Zero.

A crow flies up from roadkill: a fluffy, flat scab that was a jackal or a dog.

Jabulani interprets this as an ominous sign.

The news at noon:

RADIO: An earthquake off the island of Sumatra in Indonesia was felt as far as India and Myanmar. The force of the earthquake registered as high as nine on the Richter scale. A tsunami triggered by the earthquake has devastated the coastlines of Sri Lanka and India. The Thai islands of Koh Phi Phi and Phuket have been hit hard and the lives of scores of locals and holidaymakers have been lost. A run-up of fourteen metres was reported in Cape Coral, Thailand.

Zero's verdict: This is radical, man.

– How come such things always happen in Asia or Africa or somewhere poor?

– That's a good question, teacherman. You got me.

At that moment Zero sees a spinning blue light up ahead.

– Fuck. Roadblock.

– I thought you felt lucky, says Jabulani.

Zero just glares at Jabulani. His mind's spinning. He has something to trade but that'd just be shooting himself in the foot. And it'd be wiser to kowtow and bow his fool head than to haggle hard.

A spindly young policeman signals their convoy to a halt with his rifle.

In his mind Zero inventories the contraband they have on board: an arsenal of unlicensed guns, a hijacked army truck loaded to the hilt with dope to send him on a high for as long as Mandela spent in jail, a looted jeep, nine illegal aliens, and then there's Phoenix, a wanted killer.

Zero winds down his window.

YOUNG POLICEMAN: Your licence.

Zero winks at Jabulani. So far so good. His licence is valid.

YOUNG POLICEMAN: You travelling in convoy?

ZERO: Yessir.

YOUNG POLICEMAN: But we are not at war now.

ZERO: Hijackers, madmen, baboons, aliens.

YOUNG POLICEMAN: Funny. What do you have in the truck?

ZERO: Just shit.

YOUNG POLICEMAN: You being cocky?

ZERO: No.

The policeman calls on his radio. Before long another, older policeman saunters along.

Jabulani ducks his head to stare at his feet.

DE LA REY: You called me over?

YOUNG POLICEMAN: This coloured's acting white.

De la Rey peers into the Benz and studies Zero, then Jabulani.

DE LA REY: Freedom, my man!

Jabulani tilts his head to look De la Rey in the eyes.

DE LA REY: You travelling again?

Zero's gobsmacked.

JABULANI: Just seeing the country.

DE LA REY: It's a beautiful country, hey Freedom?

You can tell the young policeman feels let down.

YOUNG POLICEMAN: Sir, this coloured told me they got *shit* in the truck.

DE LA REY: Just be cool, sarge. I have this in hand.

He studies Zero's licence.

DE LA REY: Tell me, Zero Cupido, that *shit* of yours you say you got on board, is it good shit or bad shit?

The sarge wiggles a finger in his ear as if hoping to free it of wax.

ZERO: Good.

DE LA REY: Sarge, let them go. This Zimbo called Freedom's a teacher. He's a good man.

The sarge slinks off, sulking at being put down in front of a coloured.

DE LA REY: Hey Freedom, you heard that Pajero chick survived?

JABULANI: I saw it in the papers.

DE LA REY: I radioed folk up north to track down your marijuana farm. They never found it.

JABULANI: I think perhaps I imagined it after all.

DE LA REY: I thought so. Maybe you doped too hard? Funny thing is that chick's gone too. No longer in hospital. Magically healed, maybe.

JABULANI: That amazes me.

DE LA REY: Makes you wonder if she wasn't some kind of fairy godmother, hey? You go now. Stay off that drug. And have a good trip.

To Zero this sounds paradoxical, but he just nods ta to De la Rey and fires up the Benz.

In the rearview Zero sees the Cherokee and the troop truck following. And he sees old De la Rey waving as if seeing off his kin on a long journey.

Words elude Zero. He realises he may have to revise his view of the pigs.

He turns on the radio again:

RADIO: . . . swamped Sumatra and the Nicobar Islands and ravaged Pondicherry. The tsunami is now heading for Malindi on the east coast of Africa . . .

A good thing Zimbabwe's so far from the sea, thinks Jabulani. This is one risk in an otherwise lawless land that Thokozile and Panganai and Tendai are spared.

RADIO: And in Dhaka the cricket game between India and Bangladesh goes on despite the tsunami.

– At the end of the day, Freedom, even if half the world sinks into the sea, folk will go on playing cricket.

– Since they are not dead.

– That's the truth, brother. And by the way, all the money from this dope goes to you. To get your folk out.

Jabulani stares out at the alien, yellow veld and thinks: *Angels come in the strangest forms.*

47

Boxing Day, 26 December 2004. Hermanus. Dusk.
Vertigo blooms in my head. A gust taunts me. My toes jut
out over the void.

The tide will tug my corpse off the fanged reef of rocks below.
Sharks will filch snatches of my skin and crayfish pick tatters off my
bones as they jig and clink among the shells and stones of this whale-
song sea.

Lotte will trawl the market for word of me. Yet how am I to go
on in a world where my love for her is hung out to dry like fish on
the salting poles?

Another gust floats a line of song sung by the urchin opera-boys
singing for pennies. My hands fly out to catch the foreign words
fluttering like sparrows over my head.

A whale blows in the distant deep. I hope to see the outline of
the tail but the whale stays under.

I feel deserted. I see no hope.

Then I fall and the wind howls her mad opera in my ears.

Dassies eye me incuriously from cracks in the cliff.

I see Lotte wing by, her angel wings whistling in fight.

I call out to her, yet she, cool and alien, is focused on the flaming horizon.

Below me a freak wave flash-floods over the rocks. Cormorants shoot skyward like jagged shrapnel.

I feel a sharp sting under the soles of my feet. Now I'm tumble-turning underwater, glancing off rock, seeking the sky. I have no sense of north or south. The sea shouts in my ears.

My mind goes blank. Then I see the bare tits of that whore in Amsterdam. She tugs my head into the clammy hollow between them. I wriggle hard but she won't let me go. Zero laughs.

A sun-flared film unreels in my head: My sister and mother skip through water fanned by my thumb jammed into a hosepipe. Zero plays a frenzied salsa rhythm on his old guitar, as Cuban bands will till a girl's skirt falls off. They flash smiling teeth at me, cuttlefish white. And my sister is unaware she'll die tomorrow.

Am I now dead, I wonder?

But then I bob up and founder like an oil-lamed seagull on the raging surface.

Just as a wave wants to dash my skull against the harbour wall, a rip tide yanks me out to deep sea again.

I see the professor and his dog high on the harbour slipway. His fishing boat has been flipped over and is bobbing keel-down in the harbour.

Now the professor casts out his line of tatty string, a tennis ball tied to the end.

The ball eludes me. I go under again.

Now I see a myriad-handed Lotte dancing blue-skinned and lolling-tongued on my corpse.

And Buyu: jumping up and down on a jetty alongside a band of stray dogs capering on their hind feet, caterwauling one and all to the moon.

I surface again and catch hold of the ball. The professor reels me in, hand over hand.

On the slipway where they used to land and gut whales I feel Moonfleet lick salt and blood from my flayed skin.

In my mouth there's a salty taste of shame that I'd abandon my mother marooned and uncured and Hunter so dry and wistful and Buyu all agog and zingy.

And yet I wish a rock had ended this futile longing for Lotte, ended too all recall of the police Polaroids I found in Zero's drawer: of my sister's skin overexposed and clawed on a dune, of her hands cat's-cradled with baling wire.

The world spins. I shut my eyes.

Thumbs slide my eyelids up. The professor hovers over me. He surveys the sorry flotsam at his feet and shakes his head. Perhaps he thinks: *Was it for this that I twined and twiddled my string for so long?*

Then he gazes at the sea that took his love yet so whimsically spared me.

From the cliff high above us the hunchback blows his *vuvuzela*: a long, gutting, haunting song of love for this cruel crazy beautiful south.

OPEN ROAD
INTEGRATED MEDIA

Open Road Integrated Media is a digital publisher and multimedia content company. Open Road creates connections between authors and their audiences by marketing its ebooks through a new proprietary online platform, which uses premium video content and social media.